KU-307-067

Inventing Elliot

Inventing Elliot

GRAHAM GARDNER

Orion
Children's Books

First published in Great Britain 2003
by Orion Children's Books
a division of the Orion Publishing Group Ltd
Orion House
5 Upper St Martin's Lane
London WC2H 9EA

Copyright © 2003 Graham Gardner
Extract from *Nineteen Eighty Four* by George Orwell
(Copyright © George Orwell, 1949) by permission of
Bill Hamilton as the Literary Executor of the Estate of the
Late Sonia Brownell Orwell and Secker & Warburg Ltd

The right of Graham Gardner to be identified
as the author of this work has been asserted.

All rights reserved. No part of this publication may be
reproduced, stored in a retrieval system, or transmitted,
in any form or by any means, electronic, mechanical,
photocopying, recording or otherwise, without the prior
permission of Orion Children's Books.

A catalogue record for this book
is available from the British Library

Typeset at The Spartan Press Ltd, Lymington, Hants

Printed in Great Britain by Clays Ltd, St Ives plc

ISBN 1 84255 263 5

To my parents
With love and respect

'The object of persecution is persecution. The object of torture is torture. The object of power is power. Now do you begin to understand me?'

George Orwell, *Nineteen Eighty-Four*

Prologue

Last bell had gone. He was almost out of the gates. And then they grabbed him and marched him back, round to the changing rooms at the side of the school. Kevin Cunningham. John Sanders. Steven Watson. Any one of them was bad enough. The three together were beyond his worst imagining.

They held him with his back against the wall, pinning his arms. Kevin came up close, until his breath was on Elliot's face.

'Hello, Elliot. Were you thinking we'd forgotten you?'

He said nothing. Responding could only make it worse.

'Answer when you're spoken to.'

'No.'

'No what?'

'No – I hadn't forgotten you.'

'You're a loser, Elliot, you know that?'

'I . . . know that.'

Kevin smiled. 'There's a place for people like you, Elliot. It's called the rubbish tip. Why do you keep on turning up for school? You know we're always going to be waiting, ready to put you back where you belong.' He

I

reached forward and ripped the front breast pocket of Elliot's blazer. It hung like a dead tongue.

Then he did the same to the other pockets.

For a moment, Elliot felt nothing. Then something inside him shifted. Suddenly, terrifyingly, like nothing he'd experienced before, white-hot rage erupted. It consumed him, uncontrollable, an exploding fire-storm, lunatic fury. He tore free of the hands pinning him and hurled himself at Kevin and hit him, hit him again, again, again –

'I'll *kill* you, I'll *kill* you, *kill* you, *kill* you!'

They wrenched him off and threw him against the wall. The back of his head smashed against the tiles, and he felt sick.

Slowly Kevin got up. He wiped blood off his mouth. 'You're going to wish you never did that.'

Elliot's rage was gone. Instead, he was blissfully numb. Everything was clear to him now. He would be dead very soon. But really, they'd already killed him a long time ago. So they couldn't hurt him any more.

'You can't kill me,' he said. 'I'm already dead.'

The first punch was right over his heart, and didn't hurt at all.

You can't hurt me. I'm dead already. Dead.

But then came a second punch, in the side of his head, and a third, right where the first one had landed.

Pretty soon it did hurt.

But you can't hurt me, he thought. *I'm dead already.*

It hurt more: a spreading pattern of warm pain.

Then a thermonuclear blast obliterated the top of his head, and he was falling, down, down. And mercifully, he died.

Chapter
1

Elliot Sutton swallowed the sick, sour fear that threatened to engulf him. It was New Year's Day. Less than a week before he started at his new school.

Think positive, he kept telling himself. It was supposed to be a new beginning here. His new school had been told nothing about what had happened before. He was coming to it with a clean record, a blank identity. It would be a fresh start – as it was supposed to be for all of them.

That's a joke, he thought. As though a new house and a new town were magic spells that would get his dad well again. So far his dad had acted as if he hadn't even noticed they'd moved, settling back into the same chair, watching the same TV, day after day . . .

Think positive. Elliot looked around his bedroom at the full cardboard boxes, bulging carrier bags and the battered, open suitcase spilling clothes on to the floor. It had been two weeks since they'd moved to the new house, and he hadn't yet been able to bring himself to unpack properly. He just pulled out the clothes he needed each day and pretended to himself he'd do it 'tomorrow'.

The truth was, he dreaded unpacking. Everything in the boxes, in the carrier bags, in the suitcase, was a reminder of where he had come from – and it was a place he didn't want to go back to, even in his mind.

As he stood there, he realised that he'd made a decision without really being conscious of doing so. He wasn't going to unpack. Most of what was in the boxes and the bags belonged in his past, not the present. It should stay there. He would get out only what he absolutely needed; the rest could stay out of sight. Maybe he'd even get rid of it – that way there would be no temptation to go back to it.

He felt a surge of energy, and set to work before it faded. He emptied the suitcase on to the bed. Three pairs of jeans – they were pretty ancient, but that didn't matter. They could stay. Likewise his sweatshirts and T-shirts: One of the few compensations about staying much the same height since he was twelve was that he didn't yet need any new clothes. Which was lucky, since the last time he'd tried to persuade his mum to let him have some money to get some, she'd looked at his old stuff and exclaimed, 'What's wrong with these? There's years of wear left in all this, as long as you don't grow any!' Shorthand for, *Sorry, we can't afford it.*

The problem was school uniform. He needed trousers, a blazer, shirts, tie, games kit . . . It was going to cost a fortune. There was no way his mum could afford to buy brand new. They would have to go to the second-hand shop.

Which meant he would get noticed straight away.

He put depressing thoughts about clothes to one side, delved into the nearest box for the few books he'd brought with him, and put them on the low bookcase.

As for the rest of the stuff . . . He pulled out a dusty

photo album. The pictures in it – of him growing up, of the family: of him, Mum, Dad – were all from at least three years ago. His mum hadn't taken any photos for a long time.

He put the album back and pushed the boxes under the bed, the suitcase on top of the wardrobe.

He thought he wouldn't put any posters up. He'd have clean, bare walls. They would be a constant, pleasant reminder that this house was brand new. Fresh. As everything was supposed to be from now on. He breathed in the smell of it – the clean, heady scent of new paint and wood; held it in his lungs.

He let the idea which had been slowly germinating take fuller hold. *No one knows me here.* He had a chance. The chance not only to leave the old Elliot behind, but to invent a new Elliot. An Elliot built from scratch.

'No one knows me,' he whispered aloud.

It didn't have to be like before.

I won't let it be like before.

They'd been a happy family once.

He had to remember that.

His dad had been setting up his own business. He was going to make and sell packaging: specialist packaging for fragile and valuable goods. 'The market's out there,' he kept saying. Enough people willing to pay a lot of money to ensure that what they sent through the post didn't get damaged.

'Expensive and exclusive. That's what it's about.' His dad had kept repeating that too. Where he'd worked before hadn't been about expensive and exclusive – it had been about cheap prices and large quantities. He'd been a design assistant for a big company making packaging for other big companies. It wasn't that he hated his job, he'd told Elliot – he just didn't particularly like it. So he'd handed in his notice and started out on his own.

It had been a good time. An atmosphere of anticipation and excitement. Constant activity: his dad dashing in and out of the house, racing to finish meals, making hurried telephone calls. His dad saying, 'This is the way to go – I *know* it' at least twice a day, every day, for a year, it had seemed. And masses of extra post, envelope after envelope pushed through the letter box in the morning.

There had been lots of envelopes later, too. After a while they'd stopped coming through the letter box. Instead there would be a knock on the door, usually in the middle of breakfast, and his mum would get up, open the door, sign the clipboard held out by the postman, then come back to the table, staring at the white and brown rectangles in her hand. She never opened them in front of Elliot. She just stared, as if she couldn't quite see them properly, didn't understand what they were.

But before that . . . As soon as the letter box sounded, his dad would dash to get the post, bring it back to the table, anxiously rip open envelopes, his face creasing into a smile – or, just occasionally, a small frown – as he read.

'This is an investment in all our futures. This is for all of us.' Another of his dad's favourite phrases.

'Are you listening, Elliot my boy? This is so we can feed your book habit and still keep a roof over our heads. I saw your light on at half-eleven last night – but I don't suppose you saw our last electric bill, did you?'

This last bit he always said in a roar of mock anger. Then he'd show he was only joking by grabbing Elliot around the waist and saying, 'And I suppose you're *still* expecting me to take you to the library on Saturday . . .'

It was an old joke. He always took Elliot to the library on Saturdays, and Elliot had loved to read since as far back as he or his dad or his mum had a memory of him being able to. When he was engrossed in a book he was somewhere else, inside the story; for a short while the world left him alone.

He reached for a book now.

He tried to shut out the fear.

Happy families.

Think positive.

Chapter

2

Inventing a new Elliot took, in the first instance, money. A lot of money.

There had been one hundred and ninety-two pounds and ninety-eight pence in his savings box. Every note and coin earned by getting up early five days a week to do a paper round. All of it mentally labelled 'untouchable', waiting for the day he saw something he really wanted.

Now, as he walked around the shopping arcade, his wallet bulged with notes and change.

He could save up again for stuff he wanted. *Yeah, right.* What was important at this moment was stuff he *needed*.

Once he'd bought games kit, the school uniform came to over a hundred pounds, even though he'd been lucky enough to find a good second-hand blazer. The shoes were another forty.

After he'd bought the clothes he got his hair cut. In place of his old childish, floppy black strands he had it shaved around the sides and then bleach-streaked on top.

A new Elliot was emerging.

His wallet was a lot lighter on the way home.

It's worth it. Every penny.

His mum's reaction to the haircut and clothes was far less than he'd prepared for. The only comment she made when he came through the front door was, 'Well, if you want to waste your money, I suppose that's as good a way as any.' She didn't even mention the time and money he'd saved her by buying his own school uniform.

She looked tired. His dad was watching a football match with the sound turned up loud. They'd almost certainly had a row while he was out.

Actually, Elliot thought, 'row' wasn't the right word. A row involved more than one person, but his mum did all the shouting and crying, while his dad just sat there.

They sat down to dinner in an uncomfortable silence. Elliot swallowed spaghetti bolognese without tasting it. Everything was going to be exactly the same here, after all. Nothing was going to change.

'Hey.' His mum reached across the table and touched his arm. She smiled: a proper smile, not the worn-out grimace that was all she could usually manage. 'I got two jobs today. I've got an early morning shift cleaning at the paper mill, and I'm doing two overnights at an old people's home.'

He felt unhappy. 'How are you going to get any sleep those two days? You'll have to go straight from one job to the other.'

She squeezed his arm. 'Don't worry, I'll manage. And it means I'll be here when you come home from school.'

That doesn't matter, he wanted to say, but kept quiet – it would be throwing her efforts back in her face.

She smiled again. He noticed for the first time that her black hair contained threads of grey.

'It's going to be good here,' she said. 'I can feel it. A new start for all of us. You, me, and . . .'

She looked at his father, who glanced up from his spaghetti. Elliot tried to read his eyes. Was there something different there? The return of even a pinprick of light behind the dullness? He told himself that there was – that he simply wasn't looking hard enough.

After dinner he went into the bathroom and put on the uniform. The dark green tie looked too large on him – nothing he could do about that. But apart from that he looked OK, he thought, relieved. Looking OK was critical.

He studied his features in the mirror over the basin. The hairstyle definitely worked. It made his face sharper and older. Tougher. No longer the face of a child.

But his height (short) and build (slight) were still those of a child. He would stand out – size was one of the first things kids took notice of. He could do nothing about that.

He had just got into bed when there was a knock on the door and his mum came in. She sat on the edge of the bed – she hadn't done that since they'd moved house.

'You've got to be patient with him, Elliot. He's ill. Depression's an illness. And he's still physically damaged too. It's not his fault, you've got to understand that. We've both got to try to understand.'

'I just wish –' He stopped. He couldn't say what he wished.

She continued for him. 'You just wish it was like it was before. I know. So do I. But it's never going to be. And we're going to have to accept that.'

He looked away from her, remembering the night his dad didn't come home.

Once the business had got properly started, his dad had begun to work late almost every night. That hadn't been so great: it meant he often skipped meals at home. Elliot missed the three of them eating together, talking about nothing in particular – just being a family.

Saturdays also changed: often his dad was travelling to see a client, so he couldn't take Elliot to the library. His mum took him instead, which was fine, and once he was old enough he went on his way anyway; but somehow it wasn't quite as good as before.

But the three of them were OK. There were still Sundays, when his dad was home all day. Some evenings he left work early and it would be the same as old times, all of them sitting around the kitchen table eating, talking, laughing. And if he wasn't back for dinner, he'd come upstairs and talk with Elliot, or just say goodnight.

One night it had got very late, and his dad still hadn't arrived home. Elliot had been in bed waiting for him, half-asleep, when the front door bell had sounded. He heard the door open, unfamiliar voices, the door close again, chairs scraping across the kitchen floor under his bedroom.

He crept downstairs in his pyjamas. The kitchen door was closed.

He listened.

He couldn't hear clearly; he could just make out isolated words and phrases: '. . . assault . . . multiple injuries . . . hospital . . . operating now . . .'

Elliot had felt a growing sense of dread – the gnawing in his stomach which was soon to become so familiar. He willed the voices to continue; while they did, everything was still OK, nothing was going to change.

Keep talking. Keep talking.

Then the noise of chairs pushed back, heavy footsteps, the kitchen door opening. Two police uniforms: a man and a woman. They saw Elliot, stopped, looked at one another, nodded. The woman went back into the kitchen. The man smiled at Elliot, but it was a strained smile, as if he was having to remind himself to put it on.

'Hello there. You been listening?'

Elliot had said nothing.

'Can you go and get dressed? Your mum will be along soon.'

Elliot had carried on saying nothing, thinking *Not real. Not real. Not real.* It was something that happened only on TV: the police car outside the house, the knock on the door, the figures in uniform, the calm words and sympathetic expressions. It wasn't real life. It would only be real if he became part of it. So he wouldn't become part of it.

'Your dad's been hurt. We're taking you with your mum to the hospital, because there's no one here to look after you. OK? Your mum's just getting ready.'

Not real. Not real. Not real. Not real.

His dad had been attacked walking back to his car. Whoever it was – his dad didn't remember anything and there had been no witnesses – had taken his wallet and car keys and mobile. And fractured his skull, broken his ribs, ruptured his spleen. Left him lying on the pavement bleeding to death. Dying.

Not real. But the words didn't hold back the world any more.

'Elliot? Are you listening to me? I said, he will get better. It's going to take time, that's all.'

Visiting his dad in hospital; seeing his face swollen up like a puffball, tubes coming out of his nose, wrists and chest; watching him unable to move, hardly able to speak. Smashed.

Elliot had cried for him then. And prayed, although he didn't believe in God.

But that was three years ago. The bones had mended. His dad had come home.

Only he hadn't got better.

'You do understand, don't you?' His mum was pleading.

Elliot forced himself to look at her. 'Of course I do. I know it takes time, like the hospital said. I just wish – I just wish it had never happened, that's all.'

After she'd gone downstairs, he turned off the light, stared into the darkness. Still remembering.

He could almost hear his dad's voice, from a long time ago.

'It's a question of putting your mind to it,' he used to say – usually when they were eating dinner in the evening. 'If you're serious about something you put your mind to it, and if you put your mind to it you get it done. That's the way – that's the only way.'

And his mum smiling, saying, 'Oh yes, absolutely. Pass the salt, will you?' having heard him say it a hundred times before.

His dad would smile too, sharing the joke; but he wasn't only joking. Once, after they'd finished eating, his dad had turned to him and said, 'Listen to me, Elliot. I mean what I say. You'll always get people telling you you can't do things – telling you *not* to do things, because they can't be done, it's impossible. When I told my old firm I was striking out on my own, you know what my boss said? He said, "Good luck, you're out of your mind, we'll keep your job open so you've got somewhere to run to when you've worked it out for yourself." Can you believe that?'

Elliot had shaken his head, as he knew he was supposed to.

'That's the kind of thing you'll get, Elliot my boy, all the way through this life. But you don't listen to it. You don't listen to it.'

Well, no one was telling his dad that now, were they? No one was telling his dad 'You can't get better, it's impossible, can't be done.'

No one had been telling his dad anything like that for the past three years – exactly the opposite, in fact.

But they might as well have been.

When Elliot had said, 'I wish', what he'd meant, what he hadn't dared say, was, *I wish he'd just die.* He thought it again now, and then felt guilty and horrified at himself for thinking it.

But he didn't even really mean that. How could he want his dad to die when his dad was already dead?

The person he wanted to die was the man who sat there and said and did nothing; the man who stared silently, blankly into space; the man who wasn't his dad, however much he might look like him. If that person died, maybe his dad would come back, walk in through the front door and say –

Elliot shook away the picture angrily. *Get real! It's not going to happen. Not today. Not tomorrow. Not ever.*

But he couldn't stop imagining himself getting rid of him. Screaming at him, *Get out! Get out of our house!* Taking the biggest saucepan from the kitchen and smashing it through the TV screen and the tube imploding with a beautiful *whoomph!* and a shower of sparks.

He knew he would never actually do it – but not because he didn't dare, not because he didn't have the guts. He would never do it because he knew it would have no effect. The man in the chair – the impostor – would look vaguely at him with the same blank eyes, and then his attention would return to the box in the corner, forgetting the interruption before he'd even properly noticed it.

I hate you.

I hate myself.

And he had yet to face his new school. Less than a week away.

Maybe it was a new start.

Maybe.

Chapter
3

First day of term. Elliot approached the main entrance of his new school with a sense of foreboding.

Holminster High.

He'd visited it just before Christmas. The first thing that had leapt into his mind was an old black-and-white film he'd seen: *Goodbye, Mr Chips*. The main school was old – a huge redbrick building with sash windows. The few modern buildings were brown brick and smoked glass. All of it screamed style and good taste and expense.

His old school had consisted of a messy bundle of low towers thrown up out of pink concrete. What screamed at you there was the graffiti – the school authorities had stopped bothering to remove it, since it at least detracted from the ugliness of the architecture.

At Holminster High there was no graffiti.

There was a large expanse of neatly-mown 'lawn' at the front of the school, which in the summer became part of the playground. There were mature trees – tall, thick oaks and beeches – and flowerbeds filled with pastel-shaded perennials and delicate bedding plants. Elliot had found it hard not to be impressed.

Inside was a mixture of ancient and modern, tradition

and hi-tech. Carved wood panelling on the walls blended with textured plastic on the floors. Sepia photographs of past headmasters hung alongside abstract paintings that wouldn't have disgraced an art gallery. More style, more good taste, more expense.

The prospectus said a lot about combining 'tradition' and 'heritage' with 'dynamism' and 'forward thinking'. It also talked about 'excellent discipline', 'moral education' and 'a positive and productive environment'. Every page had at least two photographs of Holminster High pupils working earnestly, or competing in sporting events, or showing off awards and trophies.

Elliot had come away not believing it for a second. But it would be nice if the illusion persisted – even for a short while.

He let himself be carried through the school gates by the sea of red blazers.

One of the crowd. Keep it like that.

The next quarter of an hour, until form registration, could be critical. He mustn't be noticed in the wrong way.

He thought he should stay in one place, then he thought maybe he should move about. He tried to see what other kids were doing, but it was impossible to work out any pattern. Most were in small groups, some of them boys only, some of them girls only, some of them mixed. There were two separate games of footy. A few kids straggled, attached to nothing but themselves.

He moved, then stopped. Moved again. Stopped again.

His trousers itched. His collar rubbed. His shoes pinched. Sweat trickled from his armpits, although it was a cold day. He pictured it soaking into his shirt, into the crisp, clean white fabric. He was glad he was wearing a blazer.

School hadn't always been a nightmare. That was something else Elliot had to keep reminding himself. Except that it was hard to remember a time when it had ever been anything else.

His first secondary school had been OK. If he'd allow himself to admit it, he'd even quite enjoyed some aspects of it, despite everything at home. He had a small group of friends he hung around with. He didn't mind the work too much, particularly English, where they were made to write book reports. Reading for homework – that had been fine by him.

Then came the move.

With his dad in hospital and then back home but unable to work, the packaging business had gone under. His mum had taken a job at a nursing home – another step away from normal; she'd never worked before – but they still hadn't been able to afford the mortgage on the house. They had to find somewhere cheaper to live.

That might be OK, he'd thought initially, just after his mum had announced it. Not knowing, then, about the flat that was all they would be able to afford. Not knowing, then, that moving house would mean leaving the school he'd been at for less than half a term – moving away from everyone he knew.

'I'm sorry, Elliot,' his mum had said, 'really sorry. But there's no way I can afford to get you over to the other side of the city five days a week. You do understand, don't you?' Her face saying, *Please understand. Please, please, please.*

Of course he'd understood; he always understood. He was eleven years old, over halfway towards twelve, by then. Old enough not to moan. Old enough to know that it would do no good to argue.

But at the new school, somehow he couldn't be bothered. It was as if the energy, the will, the lifeforce, had been sucked out of him. Everything – thinking, doing – required a massive effort. Too much effort. He didn't try to make friends; he let his marks slip.

At his old school he wouldn't have got away with it. There the teachers had been all too ready with anxious looks, kindly-meant questions and earnest 'little chats'. But at this school, none of the teachers seemed to be bothered that Elliot couldn't be bothered. They took registration, delivered lessons, marked homework – and that was it.

In truth, he'd been almost glad they didn't care. He wanted to be ignored; he was happy to be left alone.

Except that there were others who were not happy to leave him alone.

It began with little things. Kicks on the back of his ankles as he walked down the corridor. Cuffs on his head in lessons. Casual punches as he was changing for games. He tried to ignore it, thinking that reacting would make it worse.

The violence moved up the scale: the kicks harder, the punches heavier, the cuffs more frequent.

He didn't know why they'd chosen him. Except that he was on his own.

Except that he was small and skinny.

Except that he wore an obviously second-hand uniform.

Except that he existed.

Then came the more 'personal' attention. Ordered to the park after school by Kevin Cunningham, undisputed king of years seven and eight, built like a sixth-former, already shaving at twelve years old.

'Teach you a lesson, Ellie-boy. Teach you to make fun of me. What have you been saying about me, Ellie-boy? Think you're clever, do you?'

Elliot hadn't said anything about Kevin; hadn't said anything about anyone, come to that. But it seemed that that didn't make any difference.

He wasn't going to go to the park, but Kevin had already thought of that. On the appointed day, there were four heavies waiting for Elliot at the school gate.

The fight didn't take long. Elliot hadn't punched back, working on the principle that it would just make it worse for himself. He got away with a smashed lip, aching head – from when he'd fallen backwards – and seven violent-coloured bruises spread across his chest.

He hardly noticed the pain; he was more concerned that he'd lost a button from his shirt, bled all over it, and had grass-stains and mud on his trousers. His mum had warned him he'd have to look after his uniform – 'And don't grow. We can't afford it.' He had to try and prevent her discovering the damage.

When he got back to the flat he crept past the kitchen where he could hear his mum working, and went into the bathroom to change – there was no lock on his bedroom door.

He took off his shirt. Blood had dribbled from his lip, down his neck and on to his chest. He mopped at it with a flannel, trying to avoid the bruises.

There was a knock on the door.

'Elliot? Are you all right?'

He froze. 'I'm fine.' Struggling to keep his voice from trembling.

'Elliot? What's the matter? What's happened?'

'Nothing's happened.' Why couldn't she go away and leave him alone? He reached for his T-shirt and realised he'd left it in his bedroom – along with his jeans.

His head throbbed. He felt sick.

The door handle rattled. 'Elliot, please. Open the door. I know something's the matter. Let me see you.'

He hurt all over; he must have all along; he just hadn't realised it. He felt like crying.

'*Elliot!*'

When she saw him, she looked as if she wanted to cry too. But she didn't. She examined the back of his head, insisted he took off his wrecked trousers so she could see he wasn't hiding any more injuries, then made him have a bath.

By the time he came out, she'd phoned the school and – she told him with a mixture of anger and satisfaction – yelled at both the head and deputy head. They'd argued that because the fight had been out of school hours and off school premises it wasn't their problem.

'I told them if they didn't sort it out I'd be down there to sort it out myself – and them too.'

Kevin was 'cautioned' – the word the head had used – but nothing more, since no 'independent witnesses' would say who'd begun the fight.

Elliot's life was hell from that day on.

There were no more fights, other than the one that finished it all. But what came in place of them was almost worse.

There was the whispering campaign. *Elliot stinks. Elliot wets his bed. Elliot's a homo.* Stupid, childish stuff that no one should have believed for a second. But the whispers circulated, spread, multiplied, became elaborated. Kids stared in contempt, laughed spitefully, mimed obscene acts, threatened.

In the changing rooms, and outside on the sports field, there were opportunities for far more than whispers. His games kit chucked in the showers. Mud, and worse, in his shoes. Slams in the ribs and back. Ultra-violent tackles in rugby and football that put stud imprints on his shins and smashed the breath out of him.

Other things, far more awful. Experiences too shaming to think about.

He thought that if he defended himself he'd make it worse, so he didn't. Instead he tried to become invisible, tried to become unnoticeable. If they didn't notice him, surely they'd leave him alone.

It made no difference. They *wanted* to notice him, took pleasure in noticing him, actively sought him out. In the corridors, the playground, the dining hall – everywhere. He sought refuge in the library one breaktime, but they came for him and dragged him out. The teacher on duty looked up and said in a bored tone, 'If you want to mess about, outside's the place for it.'

Only classrooms were relatively safe; the worst anyone could do there was cuff him, kick his ankles, or knock his books and equipment on to the floor and then 'accidentally' tread on them. 'Oh, sorry Elliot, was that your stuff? Didn't notice it there.'

Day after day. Week after week. Month after month. Until it was as if it had always been like this and would always be like this, for ever and ever, life without end.

He knew he wasn't the only one to be singled out. There were at least two fights a week, sometimes in the park, sometimes in the playground. He saw others subjected to what he was going through, others who had been noticed. It didn't make him feel any better; he didn't know any of them; he didn't *want* to know them.

Losers. All of us.

The only thing that made it bearable was that he could hide it.

Those who delivered the violence weren't stupid. They pushed it just short of the point where it would be impossible for his mum not to find out about it. They never put his uniform in the showers; they didn't go for his face; they left his school text books alone.

They were doing Elliot a favour, although they couldn't have known it. The last thing he wanted his mum to do was worry about him on top of everything else.

His dad had come out of hospital an invalid. His food had to be cut up for him. He couldn't take a bath alone. He couldn't even shave himself.

His mum had to help him get dressed and washed in the morning. Then she went on to her job at the nursing home, doing the same again for people forty years older than his dad. When Elliot came home from school she was usually poring obsessively over mounds of paperwork, keeping them all going.

There was no way he could tell her his problems. He didn't want to be another burden. Anyway, anything she might do to help could only make things worse.

'Promise me you'll tell me if you get any more trouble,' she said at least once a week. 'Promise me.'

He gave the same answer every time: 'I'm fine. I promise.'

'You're sure?'

'I'm sure. Really.'

Had she truly believed him? he wondered. Or had she so wanted to believe him – so *needed* to believe him – that she let herself go along with the lie?

They tried to hold on to an echo of the past. After his mum had put his dad to bed, she and Elliot sat at the kitchen table and talked, keeping alive the memory of when it had been the three of them. It became a ritual: his mum asked about his day, Elliot asked about her day. He made up stuff – incidents in lessons, jokes, anything he could think of. She always had a story about her 'old dears' as she called the residents of the nursing home.

Sometimes, in the middle of recounting a story about work, his mum abruptly stopped talking. On those occasions he had to try and make her continue. Otherwise, horribly, she started crying. He couldn't bear that, didn't know properly what to do, had to try not to watch her until she cried herself out and blew her nose and said, shakily, 'I'm sorry, I'm sorry, I'm sorry' – whether she meant for crying or for something else he was never sure.

Later, in bed, he read for hours – until two or three in the morning, even all through the night – until he couldn't hold his eyes open any longer. It hardly mattered what he was reading as long as it stopped him going to sleep; as long as it delayed the nightmares.

Even in sleep the fear didn't leave him.

He hadn't known that all that time – those endless three years – his mum had been doing two things.

First, she'd applied for 'Criminal Injuries Compensation' on behalf of his dad. If you were injured in the type of circumstances his dad had been, the government paid a set amount of money according to how badly you had been hurt. They didn't give his dad a fortune, but it was enough for the deposit on a cheap house.

Second, she'd searched for a new place to live. Somewhere away from the city and all the memories it carried. A place where they could all make a new beginning.

She hadn't told Elliot anything about what she was doing; she had wanted to surprise him once it had all been settled.

Then . . .

He pushed the memory away.

None of that matters any more.

They were starting again. All of them.

With a jolt, he heard the registration bell. He'd spoken to no one; no one had spoken to him. *Not good.* Inside, after finding his form room from the plan on the main notice board, he made his way along corridors full of kids who already knew each other and didn't so much as glance at him. *Double not good.* When the form teacher announced him as a new arrival, a few kids looked idly at him, then ignored him. *Double-double not good.*

He tried to think positive. *At least I haven't been noticed for the wrong reason.*

Yet.

It was better not to be noticed than to be noticed for the wrong reason.

Chapter
4

Unlike Elliot's old school, the headmaster at Holminster High didn't have to ask for quiet at morning assembly. As he stepped up on to the stage at the front of the school hall the quiet chatter died away.

The head looked over the silent, expectant, upturned faces and smiled. 'A very big welcome back to each one of you. And a particular welcome to anyone who has newly joined us. I know that this is going to be a good – no, a *great* – new year for Holminster High, and I also know that each of you has the potential to be part of that greatness . . .' The words poured out, smooth and easy, as if every sentence had been rehearsed to perfection. '. . . establishing and strengthening links with the wider community . . . continuing our history of academic and *sporting* excellence . . . maintaining the tradition of the school . . .'

Elliot let the words flow over him, and wondered when he would face his first test.

He knew he wouldn't have to wait long.

The first sign of trouble came at morning break.

He had been outside for a few minutes, trying to work

up the nerve to approach someone and introduce himself, when he saw a boy coming towards him. The boy looked about Elliot's age, but was slightly taller and built more solidly. He had short blond hair brushed straight forward, and sharp features that were friendly but at the same time faintly sneaky.

Not to be trusted, Elliot thought immediately. He'd come across the same expression too many times before, on people where the friendliness was a front to gain your confidence, before they –

He tried to ignore the slight sick feeling in his stomach.

'You're new, right?' the boy said.

Elliot nodded. There was nothing to be gained by not being friendly.

'So what's your name?'

'Elliot. Elliot Sutton.'

The boy raised his eyebrows. 'Elliot? Elliot as in Ellie? Isn't that a girl's name?' His tone was still friendly. He smiled into Elliot's eyes.

Elliot braced himself and smiled back. He'd expected this. If he rose to the bait, he might as well shoot himself on the spot. 'Elliot,' he said firmly. 'Elliot as in "Elliot".'

Their eyes locked, neither of them openly challenging, neither of them ready to back down. Half of Elliot was astonished that he was daring to stand his ground like this, the other half thought, *If you let this one go, you can forget it. You've got to be determined. Don't let him know you're scared.*

Abruptly the boy dropped his eyes and extended a hand. His smile, if it were possible, grew even wider. 'OK. "Elliot" it is, then. Pleased to meet you. I'm Oliver.'

Dazed, Elliot shook his hand.

The bell rang, signalling end of break.

'See you for games this afternoon,' Oliver said, and darted off.

Elliot swallowed. The taste of the small victory was soured. Games would be the real test.

It took a supreme act of willpower to get through the door of the changing room. It was horribly familiar. Every changing room was the same: the whiff of stale sweat, damp clothing and foot powder. The floor slightly sticky beneath his shoes. Boys mock-fighting, playing catch with football boots or noisily accusing their neighbour of foot odour.

He found a clear space on a bench and changed without looking at anybody – as if he didn't care if anyone was looking at him. He waited for the jeers to start. *Hey, look at Elliot. I reckon I've seen bigger on my hamster . . . Hey, you sure you're in the right changing room? The girls' is just down the corridor . . .*

He finished tying his boot laces. Incredibly, everyone seemed to be more interested in catching the football boot than in him.

The games master, Mr Phillips, appeared in the open doorway. Everyone busied themselves with whatever stage of undressing or dressing they were at, concentrating furiously on buttons and laces. The teacher came a few steps into the room. He was built like a wrestler and blocked out much of the light.

'Who the hell's making all this racket?'

Every boy kept his head down, avoiding the teacher's eyes.

'Come on! I could hear you a hundred yards away. You

should have been out of here five minutes ago. Any more messing about and I'll have you running laps around the field instead of playing rugby.'

Chance would be a fine thing, thought Elliot. He would have loved to run laps. Exercise he didn't mind. It was playing the game that he hated. Having the same ten-stone monster tackle you and fall on you six times during one match, quite obviously doing it deliberately, and the games teacher watching and doing nothing, almost certainly secretly enjoying it. Getting yelled at for fumbling a catch, when the ball was impossible to hold: cold and greasy with thick, wet winter mud.

Oliver had already gone out without so much as a word to Elliot. Elliot trotted into the cold sunlight, his chest tight, his heart already thumping uncomfortably. This was where all the acting skill he could muster could let him down in an instant.

But in the end, surprisingly, it wasn't too bad. He ran around enough to convince both Mr Phillips and the other players that he was reasonably keen and eager to handle the ball – even though he was tackled three seconds after he caught it for the first and last time.

Someone else wasn't so lucky: a gangly kid with a crop of angry red spots on his forehead and a raw-looking nose. Every other pass seemed to be directed at him. If he caught the ball he was instantly tackled, smashed into the ground again and again, until even his face was brown. A couple of times Elliot saw a sly hand press his head into the mud, as his opponent ensured he got the most of it. When he didn't catch the ball – which was usually – he got the resentful stares of the rest of his team.

When they eventually walked off the field, Elliot's team had lost 16-24. He noticed the raw-nosed boy lagging behind.

In the changing room, Elliot quickly peeled off his muddy kit and dived for the showers. He wanted to be in and out as swiftly as possible. The keener members of his side looked angry at their defeat, and he had no wish to be a potential target for their frustration.

He let the hot water power the dirt and sweat away. 'Good game,' said someone next to him. He vaguely recognised them from the morning's English lesson.

'Yeah.' Elliot injected false enthusiasm into his voice.

Suddenly the end of the shower run was blocked. He recognised his team captain, Stewart Masters, a big, burly centre-forward who played aggressively, knocking challengers aside with casual flicks of his arm. He was still wearing his rugby shorts, and glaring.

Please don't look at me, Elliot prayed. He tilted his head back to let the water flood on to his face, trying to look unconcerned. His skin felt cold although the water was uncomfortably hot, filling the narrow space with clouds of steam.

When he next looked, Stewart had gone.

Thank you, God. Elliot stepped out into the main changing area and began towelling himself dry.

'Here he is. I've got the little sniveller.'

The changing room went silent.

Elliot froze. But the attention wasn't directed at him. In the far corner of the room, Stewart Masters had hold of the raw-nosed kid, his hand twisted in the boy's hair.

Everybody else might have been clay statues. The air

was still with expectation, a stillness which somehow emptied it of smell – of bodies, sweat, damp kit, of sound – of the showers, breathing, of anything that might distract attention from whatever was about to happen.

Stewart spoke quietly into the stillness. 'Baker, you're a snot-rag. What are you?'

'A snot-rag.' The voice was flat and dead.

'Louder, Baker. I want the whole changing room to hear you.'

'I'm a snot-rag.'

'And you stink, don't you, because you never take a bath. Don't you?'

'I – I stink because I never take a bath.'

'You're disgusting, Baker. I'm polluting myself by touching you.'

'I'm disgusting.'

'Did I ask you to speak, you little maggot? You filth stain. Did I?'

Stewart let go of the boy's hair. The tension in the room remained. Everyone knew there was more to come. Elliot held his towel, covering himself; the air suddenly felt cold; there were goose pimples all over him.

Stewart continued. 'You're filthy, Baker. Get your clothes off and take a shower.'

Slowly the boy undressed, carefully placing his clothes on the wooden bench behind him. His skin had an unhealthy, off-white pallor. He looked like a ghost, or a dead body animated by some supernatural force. Naked, he walked the length of the changing room and went into the showers.

Everything else was still.

Steward scanned the room. 'I want a volunteer. Quickly, before Phillips gets here.' He pointed to Oliver. 'You. You're volunteering to man the taps.'

Clearly knowing what was expected, Oliver walked over to the tangle of pipes and wheels on the wall that controlled the flow and temperature of the water to the showers. He reached up and rapidly twisted one of the wheels clockwise.

'A nice cold shower, Baker, to clean the filth off you,' Stewart said. He pointed to another two boys. 'You and you – clothing duty, now.'

They too knew the drill: Baker's games kit followed him into the shower.

Elliot wondered how many times this had happened before – to Baker or to anyone else. Something about the whole thing gave the impression of a routine perfected from long practice.

'What the hell's going on?'

In an instant the tableau unfroze into furious activity.

The games master came into the changing rooms and went straight to the showers.

Elliot raced to pull on boxer shorts and trousers, his heart thudding.

What are you so concerned about? a little voice hissed in his head. You didn't do anything.

The games master twisted one of the knurled wheels on the wall, and the noise from the showers dropped away.

'Come out of there.'

Baker stepped into the changing rooms, his hands covering between his legs, his thin white frame shivering.

33

'Why aren't you getting dressed, Baker?' There was impatience in his voice.

The boy awkwardly half-turned back towards the showers.

'For crying out loud!' Mr Phillips' gaze swept over the room. Elliot saw Stewart staring back: brazen, challenging. He remembered noticing Stewart's name in gold leaf on the rugby roll-of-honour board. He sensed the games master weighing up his options.

The teacher turned back to Baker. 'Just get your clothes and get dressed. And hurry up.' He turned to the rest of the room. 'And the rest of you. You've got three minutes, or you'll *all* be taking cold showers.'

Elliot finished knotting his tie, shrugged on his blazer and got out before anyone could have a chance to speak to him.

Don't be noticed. But he knew it was only going to be a matter of time before he was. And then he'd be joining Baker underneath those showers.

Nothing's going to be different here. Nothing.

I was stupid to imagine anything else.

Chapter
5

The two weeks after that first day were two weeks of growing despair and fear.

He had the right clothes. He had the right haircut. He sat in the right position in class – not too near the front, not too near the back. But he knew it wasn't enough.

The years at his last school had taught him. Trying not to be noticed was doomed to failure. There were kids who spent their time searching out kids who tried not to be noticed.

He couldn't hope that he simply wouldn't be noticed, so he had to ensure he was noticed *in the right way*.

Yeah, right, Einstein. Ten out of ten for brilliant logic. Now all I have to do is work out how.

He had a theory. Getting noticed in the right way involved making yourself stand out just enough to fit in. You had to display some quality that made someone else think, *Hey, that kid's got something*. It could be charisma, or strength, or playing rock guitar, or being good at football – it could be anything. Anything that made you stand out just enough to fit in.

At his last school, he hadn't stood out like that – he'd

stood out in the wrong way. He couldn't afford to do the same here.

But he was already at a disadvantage: he was starting in Year Nine, and in the middle of the year at that. Most friendships, most alliances, would be long made.

He needed an opportunity. He needed a moment where he could make people look and see and notice him in the right way. And he needed it fast, before they looked and saw and noticed him in the wrong way.

Every day he scanned the school notice board for some kind of group he could join, a short cut to acceptance. There were any number of school societies, all calling for new members: chess, debating, choir, maths, drama . . . Once or twice he touched the biro in his pocket, then always pulled his hand away. Joining a group could prove a short cut to acceptance, alternatively it could mark him out in completely the wrong way – as a nerd, a saddo.

Stand out for the wrong reason, you're dead.

Football . . . rugby . . . tennis . . . new players wanted . . . At this place, it seemed that if you were good at sport you were classified as 'OK', at least by the people who mattered. But he always drew back from those notices, his palms greasy with fear. He couldn't do it. He didn't only hate sports, he was useless at them. Monday afternoon rugby was seventy minutes of stomach-cramping dread.

Stand out for the wrong reason, you're dead.

Then, in the third week of term, came a chance of salvation: a notice calling for boys from Year Nine and above to try out for the school swimming team.

36

He was a good swimmer – he could say that to himself as a statement of fact, not a boast. At the local leisure centre back in the city, while his friends were messing about and queuing for the water slide, he'd found more enjoyment in swimming seriously. He'd taught himself how to cut through the water rather than fight it, built up his stamina, learnt different strokes. His friends had laughed at him; he hadn't cared. They didn't know what they were missing.

He'd just never thought of it as a sport. Sport was about competition, about being aware of others and trying to beat them. When he swam, it was nothing like that – he was in a world of his own, a world free of everyone else . . .

But it was a chance to be noticed in the right way.

Maybe my only chance.

Please let my theory be true. And please let me not mess this up.

The try-outs were on Thursday after school. He arrived at Holminster baths feeling weak and sick.

The changing room was crowded. He saw several boys looking him up and down as he changed, critically assessing him, not bothering to disguise what they were doing – another reason why he hated sports. He was acutely conscious of his slight build and skinny arms and legs, although he knew there was lean muscle there as well as skin and bone. Everyone else in the room appeared to be bigger than him, and he noticed two boys with obvious six-packs. He tried not to catch anyone's eye.

There were a few not very quiet whispers: 'Hey, no sparrows allowed.' 'Somebody tell him the food crisis is in

Africa.' His stomach churning, he walked through the changing room and out on to the poolside.

He was among the first to be called. For a horrible moment he thought he was going to be sick. Then it passed. He stood with four other boys while a square-headed man in a tracksuit gave them instructions: starting gun, dive, twenty lengths racing crawl.

Elliot took up his position. His toes gripped the edge of the pool. He didn't trust himself to look anywhere but the water in front of him.

My only chance.

He pulled his goggles down over his eyes, checked they were tight. Breathed deeply, tasted the familiar, clean chemical smell of pool disinfectant. Tensed, ready for the gun. Around him the other swimmers must have been doing likewise but he was hardly aware of them, they were no longer important. The only real reality – the only important reality – was his body and the water beneath.

Suddenly he wasn't nervous any more.

I can do this.

He heard the gun fire. Then –

Piercing the pool surface. Down . . . but not too far.

Rising. Surfacing.

Cutting through the water. Fast but clean. Every part of him talking to every other part of him, a silent language he couldn't have explained to anyone who didn't already understand it.

One, two, three . . . eight . . . fifteen . . . twenty –

He touched the bar. Stopped.

Heart racing. Surging.

Slowing.

He hauled himself over the edge of the pool – and heard the tannoy announce that Elliot Sutton had been fastest of the group, and would the next five swimmers come and take up their positions.

At the end of the try-outs he was third fastest overall, which meant he had a place in Holminster High School boys' swimming team. It was as simple as that. He shook the hand of the square-headed man in the tracksuit, who turned out to be the swimming coach, and then had his fingers crushed by the grip of someone who turned out to be the team captain. Back in the changing room the only attention he received this time was friendly nods and admiring glances.

I did it. I got noticed in the right way.

He could have cried with sheer relief and happiness. He was half-afraid to respond and acknowledge the attention, in case he destroyed the moment.

As he left, someone said casually, 'Catch you next week.' He would probably have said the same to any one of the other winning candidates, but that wasn't important. What was important, what made all the difference in the world, was that he'd said it to Elliot.

Elliot walked home on a cloud of elation, repeating the words over and over: *Catch you next week . . . Catch you next week . . .* It was unbelievable. He'd done it. He was noticed in the right way.

From now on, everything would be different. He knew it.

No maybes.

It wasn't that he suddenly became a celebrity. People

didn't crowd him or cheer him when he walked down a corridor. No one asked him to join any other teams or groups. He didn't gain a hundred 'best friends'.

But he was noticed in the right way.

He was no longer the kid who looked around nervously to see if anyone was taking notice of him, and who flinched inwardly if it looked like anyone was. If anyone acknowledged him, it was in a friendly – or at least not unfriendly – way: a nod, a brief smile, a step backwards to let him pass. Someone he didn't know invited him to go bowling and introduced him to a couple of girls from his form – although they were so drunk they didn't take much notice of him.

And he had the swimming team: a place where he fitted in and was respected the same as all the other members. There were three training sessions a week, all before school, and he gladly got up early and endured the stinging shouts of the coach in return for the easy, friendly banter in the changing room and the companionship on the walk to school.

Just one thing marred it.

It had been the first morning after the try-outs. Elliot was barely through the school gates when Oliver, who hadn't spoken to him since that first day, came up to him, offered his hand and said, 'Heard about last night. Nice going.'

'Thanks.' Elliot was cautious, careful not to appear too enthusiastic. Maybe Oliver was one of those people who sucked up to whoever was flavour of the month, desperate to be liked by whoever mattered, or hoping just to be seen with them so that they could bask in their glory. Although

Oliver didn't seem like the desperate type. He had an easy, confident air, so much so as to give the impression that he didn't care whether Elliot liked him or not.

No big deal either way, Elliot thought.

There was a silence, which Oliver seemed happy to leave empty. Elliot searched for something to say. Then, before he could come up with anything, Oliver said abruptly, 'You have a problem.'

'What do you mean?' Elliot was instantly on alert, ready for trouble. He'd been caught too many times like this. *First the smile, then –*

'You have a problem, because you don't know anything.'

It was delivered as a statement of fact. Elliot was thrown off balance, not knowing how to respond. His chest tightened.

Oliver smiled. 'No one knows anything when they start at Holminster. If you're one of the unlucky ones, you get to find out the hard way – before anyone's told you. But because I like you, I'll let you in early on how things work around here. You can think of me as your helpful guide.'

His voice was still friendly, but Elliot sensed another quality, distinct but unidentifiable. It made him nervous. The little voice he'd heard in the changing room whispered, *Watch what you say from now on.*

Oliver scanned the playground, making a show of being concerned that someone might be watching or listening. Apparently satisfied, he turned back to Elliot.

'Let me tell you about the Guardians.'

Elliot felt the pulse in his neck jump, although the name

meant nothing. 'Why – why would I want to know about these . . . Guardians?'

Oliver slowly shook his head, still smiling. 'It's not a question of whether or not *you* want to know. It's a question of the *Guardians* wanting you to know. For your own . . . health and safety.'

Elliot fought down the sick feeling. He could guess what Oliver meant. 'So the Guardians are the school heavies – is that what you're telling me?'

Oliver laughed. 'I don't think so. No. The Guardians aren't the . . . heavies. You need to think of them as . . . organisation people. The Guardians *control* the heavies – although I don't think they'd like that term. The Guardians . . . organise things.

'I'll spell it out. In the classroom, the teachers have authority, OK? It's their territory. But outside, they control nothing. Nothing at all. Got it? Because out here it's the Guardians' territory. Out here, what goes is what the Guardians say goes. If a kid is getting punished, the Guardians have decided it. They select who get punished, they select who punishes. Or sometimes they'll just select the kid to be punished and let nature take its course. Know what I mean?'

Guardians . . . punishment . . . selections. Elaborate names for familiar, ugly things: heavies, violence, intimidation.

'Keep your eye on the main notice board. That's where the special selections go up. The ones you're supposed to attend. Look for a square of yellow paper.'

Elliot thought he was expected to say something. He tried to sound calm, tried to show that he wasn't bothered, wasn't impressed. 'Sounds pretty neat. I guess it isn't always that simple, though? I mean, what if someone decides they just want to beat up on someone?'

Oliver said simply, 'That's not the way it works around here. We're not like a lot of schools. You'll find that out pretty soon.'

Again, Elliot felt that it wasn't a threat, but again something in Oliver's tone unsettled him.

The first bell sounded. Oliver ignored it.

'What you need to remember is this. When the Guardians select a kid, that kid's been asking for trouble. You don't get selected for doing nothing. Like I said – we're different at Holminster.'

Elliot thought of the raw-nosed kid – what was his name? Baker? – in the changing room. He supposed you could say kids like that were always asking for trouble . . .

Except that that wasn't right, didn't properly describe what it was.

Not *asking* – that was the wrong word. It was more like . . . *waiting*.

Some kids *waited* for trouble. They weren't noticed because of anything they did or said; they were noticed because they didn't pretend to be anything other than what they were. They never looked like anything other than losers, victims, easy meat. They *waited* for nature to take its course.

Elliot knew it because he knew the way *he* had looked, the way *he* had behaved. His face, his body language, everything about him had emitted the same signal: *I'm waiting. Come and get me.*

It was what *they* looked for.

He shuddered inwardly.

Still Oliver hadn't moved. Everyone else had gone inside.

Elliot wanted to get away from Oliver but he didn't want to show his fear, which trying to leave would surely do.

He said, 'So do these Guardians have names? Who do I have to look out for?'

Oliver looked at him sharply. 'Why's that important? If I were you, I'd just make sure there was never a reason for *my* name to find its way to the Guardians. Know what I mean?' He turned and walked away.

Not a threat – a warning. Elliot realised now that it had been there all along: it was the nagging quality he'd previously failed to recognise beneath Oliver's bland voice and bland smile. Oliver knew more – maybe a lot more – than he was letting on; was possibly even one of these Guardians he was talking about. And he wanted Elliot to know it.

Why? Because he liked to show off? Or something more sinister – a coded message, Oliver's way of saying, *You don't fool me. However hard you try to pretend you're someone else, I'll always know who you are.*

Elliot discovered he was shaking.

I'm not safe here. Not here – not anywhere.

Several weeks on, Oliver's warning was fading in Elliot's mind.

If the Guardians existed, they were so secret as to be invisible. Although Elliot didn't know anyone well enough to ask about the Guardians outright, he had watched, listened, waited for even a whisper of the name.

Nothing. No one mentioned them. No piece of yellow paper appeared on the notice board.

He began to think that maybe Oliver had invented the whole 'Guardian' thing. Maybe he did it with all new kids – made himself out to be some sort of gangster in an attempt to look big. All that stuff about 'punishments' and 'selections' could be straight out of a film. He'd tried to speak to Oliver again, but whenever they crossed paths, Oliver always made out he was on his way somewhere: 'In a hurry,' 'See ya around,' 'Catch you tomorrow.'

Elliot became aware that he was breathing more easily, watching and listening with less concern. His theory had been right. If you were noticed in the right way, you were OK. No one at Holminster High was after him.

They were after others.

The raw-nosed kid.

A kid with a stutter.

A kid whose hair looked as if it had been cut by his mum.

Two kids from Elliot's form, who always hung around together at breaktimes.

Fat kids.

Little kids.

Elliot hadn't noticed to begin with, but gradually he saw.

In the playground. Small huddles of boys drifted apart, leaving behind someone sprawled on the ground, or crouched down, or bent over, uselessly clutching an injured hand, leg, arm, belly, groin.

In the corridor. In the classroom. Casual movements brought fists, feet and elbows into hard contact with soft flesh, producing little sounds of agony, quickly cut off.

Subtle violence.

But they aren't after me. They notice me in the right way.

It seemed possible, for the first time in three years, that there might come a time when he didn't have to be scared any more.

Also for the first time, school was almost preferable to home. His mum seemed to be tired all the time – too tired to talk to him, anyway. The most Elliot usually got out of her was a strained smile. They ate in silence.

A few times he woke in the early hours of the morning and heard his mum crying downstairs. He tried to shut out the sound. He thought she just wanted to be left alone; that was the impression she gave most of the time now.

He began to hate going home.

As he walked out at morning breaktime on the first day back after half-term, nodding to someone he recognised, he had no reason to think that anything was going to change.

And then everything changed.

Chapter
6

Someone grabbed his arm.

It was Oliver, excited, his face flushed. He pulled at Elliot like an impatient child. 'Come on! We'll be late.'

'What are you talking about?' Unwillingly Elliot walked faster. 'Late for what?'

Oliver pointed. 'Late for *this*. Late for the *punishment*.'

Elliot followed Oliver's finger, and saw a crowd surging towards the toilet block. Instinctively he checked to see if any teachers had noticed the movement and were already coming over. He couldn't see a single one. That had been a joke at his old school: Why are teachers like buses? Because when you need one they're never around, and then three come along at once.

'Come *on*,' Oliver insisted.

Elliot found himself running with a strange and horrible sense of urgency. He had no desire whatsoever to find out what was happening, but refusal or hesitation would mark him out in Oliver's eyes.

At least thirty boys had crammed into the small build-ing. Oliver pushed through them, tugging Elliot along with him. Nobody protested.

He found himself on the edge of a rough semicircle in

front of the toilet cubicles. The crowd pushed against his back, eager and impatient. Its excitement spilled over in a continuous roar of noise, which in the confined space was deafening.

His stomach churned. It was hard to breathe, the air thick and glutinous, over-heated by the mass of bodies. But it wasn't just that. The mingled smells of stale urine and harsh disinfectant conjured up unwanted memories. He knew what was going to happen here. He had to get out.

He pushed back against the crowd, but it was a solid mass, immovable. He was trapped. He felt his memories, his past, break out, rear up, prepare to strike.

As if someone had flicked a switch, a hush fell.

'Coming through,' a voice called.

The crowd parted, admitting three people to the semi-circle. Elliot recognised one of them from rugby, although he didn't know his name – one of the giants who got angry when he lost. The other looked slightly older, with short, spiky brown hair.

They held the arms of the third boy. Alongside them he seemed ridiculously small, like a cloth doll shrunk in the wash. His uniform was immaculate: the shirt crisply white, the tie perfectly knotted, each trouser leg with a knife-edge crease. He looked straight ahead, occasionally blinking, his small face very pale.

He was trying very hard, Elliot knew, not to look scared.

The crowd waited, silent.

The boy Elliot recognised gazed around the audience, smiling, stroking his jaw.

He's doing this deliberately, Elliot thought, his stomach bucking against his ribs. Playing to the crowd, cranking up the tension. He swallowed fear. *For God's sake get this over with.*

Without warning, the second boy turned and kicked open the door to the middle toilet cubicle. It banged against the thin partition wall, the noise shockingly loud. He turned back and pointed to someone on Elliot's right. 'You do his blazer,' he ordered. He pointed to someone else. 'You get his trousers.'

Elliot couldn't watch, but he had to. And as he watched, he couldn't hold down the past any longer. It reared again and struck, struck again, again, pounding him, ripping into him. Until he couldn't tell the difference between what was happening now and what was happening *then* . . .

. . . A mob of fighting hands wrenched his trousers down below his knees, ensuring he couldn't kick anyone, then pulled his blazer down to his elbows, stopping him lashing out. He was helpless, incapable of resistance.

They dragged him to the toilet. *'Get him in there . . . Drown the little runt . . . Make him scream . . .'*

Hands on his neck, his head forced down into the stained white porcelain bowl. The stench of disinfectant and stale urine suddenly much stronger, biting into his nose and throat. The coldness of the bowl, the side of his face rammed hard against it.

Then the choking and spluttering that signalled the flush. The water boiling up, forcing itself into his nose, his eyes, his ears. *Can't breathe.* Swallowing, gagging, choking on the taste and force of it.

Being let up for air – wrenched up by his hair, his

tormentors not wanting to risk getting anything on their own skin – gulping in deep. Being forced down again and again, sometimes five or six times, depending on how bored or angry they were.

Hating himself, despising himself for allowing it to be done to him.

Hating himself, despising himself, for allowing it to be done to someone else.

He tightened his insides until he couldn't breathe, so that his horror and fear and disgust and self-pity wouldn't show. His fists clenched tighter and tighter, until his knuckles burned, until his nails gouged into his palms.

Stop it. Stop it. Just stop. Stop.

It took six flushes before people began getting bored and started to drift away.

Oliver had disappeared somewhere into the crowd. Elliot forced himself to hold back, letting bodies flow around him. He couldn't just go. What if the kid was hurt? He couldn't –

The other part of him screamed, *Get out of here! What do you think you can do? You'll wreck everything.*

But everyone else was gone. There was no one to see him, no one to care. Including whoever had been 'punished'.

He noticed a small black canister lying on the floor, just inside the middle toilet cubicle. He picked it up. Inside was a roll of film. Someone must have dropped it. It was hard to imagine either of the two punishers as photographers, which meant it had to belong to the small kid.

He didn't want to have anything more to do with what had happened, but he couldn't bring himself to throw the canister into the bin. There might be important stuff on the film. Besides, even if there wasn't, he couldn't help feeling that it would somehow be . . . *wrong* to destroy it. He dropped it into his blazer pocket.

Outside, he glanced up at the blank windows over-looking the toilet block. He realised with amazement that they had to belong to the staffroom. How was it possible that not a single teacher had noticed what had been going on? At break the staffroom would be crammed with teachers. They would all have to be either blind, incredibly unobservant, or . . .

Or they were scared. Or they simply didn't care. Exactly the same as at his old school. Up there they were safely out of harm's way, in their cosy room that stank of fag smoke and cheap coffee. Here they didn't have the stupid notice they'd had at his previous school: 'Unless emergency or National Lottery win, go away!' in big red print. But it was just the same. Holminster had smoked glass and oak panels, while his old school had chipped concrete and torn-up plaster – but inside they were identical.

There was no escape. No escape – ever.

The night was quiet. Elliot lay in bed unable to sleep.

Images and fragments of conversation looped endlessly inside his head. The kid in the toilets, his head held under again and again, the water flushing again and again. *You don't get selected for nothing.* Oliver's face, his skin flushed with excitement. His own breathing, ragged with fear. Sweat beading above his upper lip. Noise. Heat.

Can't breathe.

He turned on to his back, struggling to get comfortable.

He stared at the ceiling. Occasionally, when a car passed, stray light from the headlamps patterned it with swirls and shadows. But otherwise it was blank. Not at all like his bedroom in the flat, where a bloom of wet mould had been spreading across the ceiling from one corner, turning the surface into a complex fabric of blacks and dirty greens. Elliot had got into the habit of charting its progress, waiting for each glare of headlights and then checking to see if the mould had grown since the last time. Some nights he'd lain awake for hours, listening intently for the sound of an approaching car, making sure he made use of every bit of light.

Other times he stayed awake for other reasons. There wasn't only the noise of the cars to wait for. There were the drunken yells, the shouted obscenities – sometimes from a distance, other times sounding so close they might be under his window. And there was the metallic smash of breaking glass – lots of different types. After a while, you learned the difference between bottle, car headlight and window.

He lay there listening, imagining, wondering if it was safe to go to sleep. There were three bolts on the door to their flat – although it was against fire regulations – and two bolts on the ground floor door to the whole block. But the windows were easy targets, fragile, no protection from what was out there in the dark.

No . . . No, that was then. Not now.

He listened. The night was quiet, the same as every night here, even Fridays and Saturdays. But it was still hard to get to sleep. The silence was unnerving, as if something was waiting to happen, waiting to explode into noise and violence. And with nothing to listen to, he couldn't get today out of his head. *Get his trousers. Duck him. Drown the little runt.*

No . . . No, that, too, was then. Before. Not now. He opened his eyes wide, trying to blank out the images.

No way I could have got involved today. Nothing I could have done.

The bed was too hot, claustrophobic. His body itched madly, the duvet burning his skin. He threw it off, and for a few minutes had peace. He shut his eyes, only for the images and sounds to return. But this time it wasn't him watching; he wasn't a spectator . . .

He blinked back warm shame, remembering the foulness and his utter humiliation; remembering being finally abandoned, vomiting on to the floor to the sounds of retreating laughter. Today had been like living it all over again, even though he'd only watched.

He was ashamed of himself for watching, and for feeling only useless pity for whoever had been punished. But most of all, he was ashamed for not being able to stop himself thinking, *If it's someone else, at least it isn't me.*

He knew he was crying for himself, not for anyone else.

Chapter
7

Every few days a new square of yellow paper appeared on the notice board. It was as if the first punishment had signalled the end of a ceasefire, the end of a temporary suspension of the worst hostilities. Part of Elliot wondered why there had been the period of quiet at all. The rest of him didn't want to think about it – any of it.

When he saw a new name go up, he stayed in the library at breaktimes, hoping that Oliver wasn't looking for him. A few times he looked out and saw a crowd running towards the toilet block; other times it headed in the direction of the cricket pavilion or the groundsman's hut. He closed his mind against it.

He only wished he could close his mind – and ears and eyes – on Monday afternoons. Since he'd become caught up in the punishment in the toilet block, the weekly ritual had become somehow much worse: he hadn't been able to ignore it so well.

Whichever team lost or won a match, the result for the raw-nosed kid was always the same: the quiet lash of abuse, then being made to stand under the cold shower while his games kit was tossed in after him. But it wasn't just the fact that it happened that made it so awful. The worst part of it was the atmosphere of inevitability. Everybody expected it to happen. Everyone waited for it to happen. And when it happened, nothing disturbed the routine. Nobody protested. Nobody spoke. Some boys watched quite openly. Others apparently concentrated on getting dressed, but usually they watched too, furtively. A few blatantly enjoyed it, but with most of them it was impossible to tell what they were thinking.

Elliot always tried not to watch, focused on dressing as fast as possible, hoped that no one was watching *him*. He lived in fear that one day he would be called on for shower or clothes duty. He didn't know what he'd do then. But whatever he did, it was impossible to escape it. Whatever you were doing, you were part of it. If you were there, you couldn't not be.

Just as when you were elsewhere – in the playground, between classrooms, walking home, using the toilets – you couldn't not be part of what went on, couldn't not be aware of the subtle violence, couldn't not sense the tension and expectation.

Somewhere, behind all of it, were the Guardians. He no longer doubted their existence.

Any sense of safety was gone. He lived in constant fear of discovery, of being noticed in the wrong way. But whereas at one time he would have waited for it to happen, now he redoubled his survival tactics. He developed, with the aid of a mirror, an expression of calm unconcern, so that no one could read what he was really thinking. In any situation he could adjust his face to communicate appar-ent bored indifference. He attended swimming practices, doing his bit to 'serve the spirit of Holminster High'. He kept up with school work but tried not to get too many high marks, in case he got praised in class. He did everything that would make him noticed enough not to stand out, stand out enough not to be noticed.

Outside he was Elliot the Indifferent, but inside he was a churning mess of violent emotions and sensations. He began to sleep badly again, waking every few hours in a sweat of terror, torn out of dreams where past and present re-played themselves endlessly, over and over.

Whatever he did, wherever he went, it made no difference. It seemed he'd always be in the same place: fear's territory.

He needed all his concentration for the game. Mr Phillips was in an ugly mood, looking for trouble, looking for someone to pick on.

He was given his chance ten minutes into the first half. The raw-nosed kid, Baker, was thrown a pass. Amazingly, he caught it – and then the mud-smeared ball slipped through his hands, to be snatched up instantly by a member of the opposing team. A second later the whistle shrilled, calling a halt to play. Both teams waited nervously, unsure of the reason for this pause.

The games master went straight up to the raw-nosed kid. Elliot felt the tension evaporate.

'What do you think you're playing?' The teacher loomed over the boy who instinctively backed away.

'I said, what the hell do you think you're playing? Haven't you had a ball thrown at you before?'

Looking at the ground the boy said something, too quiet for Elliot to hear.

'Too right you dropped it. You're wet, Baker, that's your trouble. What are you?'

The reply was inaudible.

'Louder. Everyone wants to hear you. Come on.'

'I'm wet.'

'Louder.'

'I'm wet.'

'Louder. Say it like you mean it.'

'I'm wet. I'm wet. I'm wet.'

The games teacher stepped back. 'You don't need to tell us that, Baker. I think we've all worked it out for ourselves.'

Several players sniggered.

'You don't like rugby, do you?' The games master continued to speak loudly, obviously for the benefit of everyone listening. His voice took on a mocking tone. 'You'd rather be nice and warm and all comfy; you'd rather be inside, where you can't get all horrid and dirty and bruised. Away from the horrid rough lads out here on the rugby field. You'd like that, wouldn't you, Baker?'

He turned to the waiting players, who by now were making no attempt to conceal their enjoyment. Elliot had a suspicion that this wasn't the first time the raw-nosed boy had been singled out like this.

The games master smiled wolfishly. 'This tender little lad is too delicate to play on the rugby field, so I'm left with deciding what exercise he should be taking instead. Has anyone got any bright ideas?'

A boy next to Elliot called out, 'Put him with the girls, sir. Make him play netball with the girls.'

Mr Phillips' smile widened. 'An excellent suggestion, Harris, thank you.

'So, Baker, what are you waiting for?'

Elliot's team was thrashed, losing 8-30. Back in the changing rooms Stewart was in a vicious mood, dragging the raw-nosed kid across the floor by his hair. Two boys had hold of his clothes. Oliver's hand was on the shower wheel. Everyone else watched in silence.

Suddenly, without warning, the games master walked in. The drama froze. No one looked anywhere. The only sound was the gush of the showers.

Mr Phillips took in everything. His eyes rested for brief eternities on the boy on the floor, passive and immobile, and on Stewart, whose fingers were still, as if by accident, gripping the boy's hair.

Thoughts raced through Elliot's mind. Why had Phillips come in? Coincidence? Or had someone tipped him off?

Still no one moved. The showers were a torrent of noise.

The games master's eyes came to rest on Elliot. 'You.' He walked up close to him. 'I don't know you, so maybe I'll get a half-truthful answer. What do you have to say about this?'

When Elliot thought about it afterwards, the most frightening thing was how easily the lies formed in his mind, how natural it was to say them. But then, at that moment, he was hardly conscious of lying. He was aware of the closeness of the games master, of his aggression. He was aware that it was undirected aggression, that the teacher wasn't interested – or didn't want to know – what was really going on, but would be satisfied by any reasonable answer. And he was conscious of how the other boys in the changing room were very deliberately not looking at him. They were making it clear that *he* was to choose what answer he gave.

It was a clear choice: an answer that would at minimum mean a detention for everyone directly involved, and probably everyone in the room, or an answer that would mean the games master yelling at them for making him have to come in to find out what might be going on. In fact, it was hardly a choice at all . . . and it wasn't as if anything had actually *happened* – Stewart had been interrupted . . .

He said, quickly, 'It was just someone messing around, sir.' He caught Oliver's face. 'And the showers were too hot, so . . . Nothing happened really, sir.'

He had an anxious few seconds while Mr Phillips stared at him with mistrustful eyes, but he'd judged correctly: the games master wasn't interested in more than a plausible explanation. He stepped away from Elliot and glared at the half-dressed figures irritably.

'If I hear a single solitary *whisper* after I go out this door, the last thing you'll be worrying about is the heat of the water.' He glanced with unconcealed dislike at the boy on the floor, then strode out, leaving the door open.

Later that night, Elliot lay in bed staring at the ceiling, his mind slowly turning. He knew that something important had taken place in the changing room. Something within him. It was not that he had never lied before, but this had been different. The instant he had said those words – the lies – he had crossed a line. And the crossing fundamentally divided everything he had done up to that point from whatever he might do after.

He knew it was a defining moment.

Chapter
8

He was barely out of the school gates on Tuesday when Oliver stepped from nowhere.

'The Guardians want you.' Oliver said it matter-of-factly.

Elliot's stomach kicked. Cold tendrils of fear coiled around his chest. He swallowed and braced himself. Outwardly he had to appear composed and unconcerned.

'When?'

'Now.'

There was no point in asking 'Why?' Even if Oliver knew he probably wouldn't say. Not that it mattered, anyway.

Elliot considered ignoring the command, shrugging Oliver off and walking home anyway. There was nothing to stop him. Except that it was the same as when he'd been told 'Up at the park,' at his old school. Oliver would already have planned for the contingency. It was better to get it over with, not make them angry.

To his surprise, Oliver led him around to the back of the school and then headed into the woods that came up close to the playing fields.

He'd never been in the woods before. It was very quiet.

Occasionally a bird chattered, always some distance away. The air was dank and chill-cool, completely different from the crisp, dry cold outside. There was a reek of acid decay from rotting leaves and vegetation, and at every step his shoes sank into mud and slime. It was a proper fairytale wood: not the nice sort with rosy-cheeked grandmothers and friendly dwarves, but the sort where unpleasant things lurked in the darkness.

Somewhere amongst all this the Guardians waited for him.

The coldness in his chest intensified and spread.

They walked without talking. The path they followed was well-trodden, but wound through the trees in no obvious direction. To make everything worse, it was rapidly getting dark. Very soon there would be nothing left even of the weak, grey afternoon light that seeped through the trees. How were they going to find their way out? Then again, *That might be the last thing I have to worry about.*

Abruptly they came out of the trees.

There was enough light to see easily. They were in a clearing: a rough circle of trampled, semi-frozen mud, about a third of a football field in size. At the far end, incongruously, was a railway embankment, running on into the trees either side. It couldn't belong to the main line – that, he knew, ran the other side of town. He wondered if trains still ran on this one.

But he quickly forgot about railways.

The embankment was fronted by a low brick wall. On it sat three figures, their legs dangling. Elliot couldn't see their faces from this distance.

Approximately two metres from the wall, Oliver stopped walking and motioned Elliot to do the same. He bowed his head. Uncertainly, Elliot copied him. Horrifyingly, he felt a sudden, burning need to pee. He fought the desperate urge to excuse himself and run for a tree. Very slowly the need subsided.

He stood for what felt like years. Now that he wasn't moving, his legs and feet were cold. The pressure on his bladder grew again, and he had difficulty concealing his discomfort. Only the thought of what might happen if he didn't enabled him to stay still.

Eventually a voice said, gently reproachful, 'Aren't you going to introduce us?'

His face blazing red, Oliver hurriedly identified the figures. The one who had spoken, on Elliot's right, was Richard. The one in the middle was Gareth; on the left, Cameron.

As soon as Oliver had finished, Richard flapped a hand. 'You can go now, Oliver.'

'Oh. Right,' Oliver said eagerly. His usual cheerful but sly confidence had gone. He was nervous, anxious to please. He slipped away into the woods.

Elliot was alone with the Guardians.

He looked at them properly for the first time. None of them fitted the mental pictures he'd created. He'd imagined them, using his old school for a model, as things close to human demons: evil with shaved heads, leather jackets and an aura of violence. What he saw was three older boys, in Holminster High School uniform, with the crest on the tie that showed they were sixth-formers. Nothing demonic. Entirely ordinary.

The one closest to him, Richard, had the easy good looks of a model. His wavy dark brown hair curled back over his ears, framing a lightly tanned face. In defiance of school regulations he had long sideburns, carefully trimmed and shaped.

Richard's eyes flicked casually over Elliot. They seemed hardly to notice him, made it clear that they didn't *need* to notice him, and yet Elliot had the idea that the older boy was filing away every detail of him. He imagined it was the gaze of someone who could afford not to care about anyone or anything. Someone with absolute confidence, absolute power.

Gareth and Cameron were also studying him, but with nothing like Richard's intensity. Elliot realised he had seen all three of them before, staring out from the pages of the school prospectus. *Sporting excellence.*

He mentally summed up and reached a decision. Richard was the most important one. The one he had to do most to appease. The dangerous one. He was faintly stunned that he was able to think rationally. The old Elliot at this point would have been ready to blubber, expecting the worst and unable to conceal it. But the new Elliot, although terrified, could hide that terror. This Elliot could appear for all the world indifferent to everything.

The way he was thinking and acting was new to him. It frightened him, though he didn't know why.

You'll get used to it. You'll learn to like it.

I hope so.

He waited.

Richard jumped off the wall. He came up close to Elliot and stooped so that their faces were on the same level. His eyes were wide, unblinking and unmoving. They gave Elliot the impression that Richard was weighing him up, evaluating him.

Perhaps Richard was something worse than a demon. A ripple of cold travelled down Elliot's back. He forced himself to hold the older boy's gaze.

Abruptly Richard straightened and stepped back. He focused on Elliot, as if seeing him for the first time.

'Why did you come out here?'

He sounded genuinely interested, not threatening, but Elliot had been through similar routines too many times to be taken in. Richard would keep up the apparent interest, even friendliness, for as long as he wasn't bored, and then it would be *Wham! In with the boot.* There was nothing to do except play along.

'I thought – I thought you asked me to.'

'Do you do everything you're asked?'

Elliot's mouth started to answer, *No*, but the word froze on his lips. Into his head came the same voice that had hissed at him before. *Remember: you have to think differently. So think differently.*

He thought, then said, terrified, 'I do things I'm asked – when I'm interested. If I want to.'

The older boy smiled. 'So why did you want to come here this evening?'

Why? Oh God, think. His mouth was dry. 'I wanted – I wanted to find out more about the Guardians.'

'Really?' Richard's smile broadened. 'So you think you know something about us *already*?'

He swallowed. 'I know some things.'

'Tell me.'

'I know that everybody's afraid of you.'

Still smiling: a mocking twist of the mouth, teeth exposed, reminding him of another smile, another person, another time. 'So are you afraid, Elliot?'

I'm not afraid. I'm terrified. He couldn't answer. Anything he said would be wrong. You could never win. In this sort of game the future was already decided. He'd been dead since the moment they'd selected him.

He waited. His stomach contorted.

Somewhere a bird chattered.

He waited. Any moment.

He waited –

He realised with a jolt that Richard was talking again.

'. . . tell us more of what you know about the Guardians, Elliot.'

How am I still alive?

There was no time to think. He lunged at the unexpected gap and blurted out what little he remembered Oliver telling him about selections and punishments. When he'd finished, he took a deep breath. It made him feel worse.

Richard closed his eyes and said dreamily, 'Not entirely inaccurate. But why do we organise all this? Can you tell me *that*?'

Elliot left unsaid the answer fluttering at the back of his mind: *There isn't a reason. Not a good one, anyway.* 'Er . . . money? Extortion, protection rings, that kind of thing?' There had been rumours of that at his old school, although it was about the one thing he hadn't been subject to.

Richard's eyes snapped open. He looked amused. 'Extortion is so unoriginal. All that kind of stuff's for the no-brainers, the thickies. They're welcome to it – outside Holminster. But they simply don't get the point of the whole exercise.' He paused, then said lightly, 'Do you get the point, Elliot?'

What was the correct answer? *Think, for God's sake.* 'The point . . . The point is . . .'

What the hell is the right answer?

Richard looked at his watch. 'It's getting late. You can go now. But think about it; *think about the point.* Got that?'

Elliot nodded, dazed, unable to speak.

'Get going then. And think about our next meeting.'

For the next four days he existed in a state of torment, the thought of the next meeting eating away at him. Obsessively, he went over and over what had happened in the woods.

Are you afraid, Elliot?

He hadn't been able to answer, and yet he was still alive. He was still dazed; could still hardly believe he had escaped without so much as a mark. He didn't know how he had dared to speak to them – to Richard – in the way he had. It was as if it hadn't been him, Elliot, in the woods at all. As if someone, something, had taken over his body.

But it's you, Elliot. You did it. No one else.

What did they want with him? He was now half-convinced that he hadn't been selected for punishment. But maybe that was what they intended him to think. Maybe it was part of an elaborate softening-up process.

Do you get the point, Elliot?

What the hell was the right answer?

★

On Friday afternoon Oliver was there again, waiting outside the school gates. He didn't need to say anything. Mutely, Elliot followed him into the woods.

This time Richard remained seated on the wall, so that Elliot had to crane his neck in order to look at him.

'We were very impressed by your behaviour on Monday, Elliot. A very cool piece of work. You more than lived up to our hopes.'

Elliot froze. There was only one thing they could be talking about: what had occurred in the changing room. How did they know about it?

'We've – *noticed* you, Elliot. You are not – how shall I put it? – you are not one of the crowd.'

Elliot's throat contracted, until he felt he was slowly suffocating.

Stand out in the wrong way, you're dead.

'You stand out from the crowd, Elliot. But not because you can't help it – that would be nothing special. When you want to be, you are part of the crowd, others accept you. A valuable skill, to be able to do that. But when you don't want to be part of it, you choose not to be. You are *able* not to be. And people accept that too, even if they don't notice it, as we do.'

Elliot struggled to understand what Richard was saying, not knowing if he was supposed to respond.

'Oh yes, Elliot. We've been watching you. For quite a while.'

How? Who? he thought wildly.

Richard laughed. 'Oh, not us personally, Elliot. We don't have the sort of low-grade minds that get excited following people around.' He adjusted a shirt cuff. 'No, we let other people do that. You really wouldn't *believe* how eager some people are. You should listen to them: they're always so busy, so anxious not to miss any little titbit. All you ever hear them saying is, "Catch you around . . . catch you later . . . tomorrow . . ." '

This time Elliot couldn't stop the spasm of expression reaching his face.

Richard laughed again. 'Don't let on that you know – you'll ruin his only reason for living.' He paused. 'Do you fancy a job like that, Elliot? Do you picture yourself watching people for us, reporting back on their every move? Who their friends are, what marks they get – well done on your last history essay, by the way; old Higgins is stingy with the B-pluses – what deodorant they use, what dirty little secrets they have . . .'

The comment on the history essay knocked Elliot sideways. Oliver wasn't in his history class. Who else was watching? Ten kids? A hundred?

Quickly he recovered himself. The remark about the essay had been thrown in carefully. Richard must have worked out precisely what effect it was likely to have. Most likely he was relying on it to scare him into taking anything else on faith. Well, he realised with surprise, he was tougher than that. Keeping his nervousness in the pit of his stomach, he said, 'It's a shame you couldn't find a more recent example. I've had two English essays since then.'

Gareth flushed. 'Watch your mouth, Elliot. We don't like smart mouths around here.'

For a moment Elliot thought he'd gone too far. But after a few seconds – enough for Elliot to know that he'd been warned and wouldn't be warned again – Richard continued.

'Well matched. Touché. We didn't really have you down as Watcher material. You have promise far beyond that.'

It was like a game, Elliot thought. A vastly complicated game, and he had to guess the rules as he went along. But he still had no real idea why he had been selected to play. It seemed as if Richard in some way approved of the fact that he 'stood out from the crowd' – but he couldn't even be sure of that. Nor was it clear what the stakes were.

When Richard spoke again, every trace of humour had been erased. His voice was quiet yet hard. 'So. On to the real business of the day. The question I left you with: the answer, please.'

The clearing was still.

For some reason, a scene flashed up inside Elliot's head: the games master humiliating the raw-nosed kid in front of everyone. Smiling . . . a wolfish grin . . . enjoying himself . . . He picked up on the thought and suddenly, wonderfully, the answer came to him.

He said, 'The point is – The point is to have fun. That's the point.'

Richard's eyebrows twitched. 'Very good. You had me worried for a moment. Do you read much?'

The abrupt change in tack threw Elliot off balance. 'Er – some. A bit.' It would have been risky to tell the truth. He didn't imagine that saying *Yeah, I read to escape people like you* would win him any favours.

'You should read more. It broadens the mind.' Richard

gave no sign that he was joking. 'Have you read *Nineteen Eighty-Four*? George Orwell?'

Elliot was thrown again, but this time only momentarily. *He's doing this deliberately,* the voice said. *It's part of the game.* More confident, even daring, he said, 'Never heard of it.' The truth this time.

'Tut, tut!' Richard shook his head, as if in sorrow. 'What *do* they teach children in school nowadays?' He reached into his blazer pocket and pulled out a battered paperback. 'Let me tell you about *Nineteen Eighty-Four* – the best book ever written, in my humble opinion. *Nineteen Eighty-Four* is about *watching*. A society where everyone is watched. In this society, there are television screens everywhere – but they aren't like normal televisions. They work both ways: you watch them and they watch *you*. They're in the streets, in the shops, where you work, in your house . . . Anything you do – maybe *everything* you do – someone is watching you.'

The story sounded vaguely familiar. He remembered a film – something about a man who was on television twenty-four hours a day.

'The next question I have for you, Elliot, is this: What's the point? What's the point of watching people all day long?'

What had happened in the film? He couldn't remember. But it was pretty obvious when you thought about it. 'To control people.' He said it indifferently, to make the fact he thought it was obvious clear. 'If people know they're being watched, they're less likely to misbehave. It's the same as the CCTV cameras in an arcade.'

Richard nodded. 'Very good.' He was serious again, the faint mocking note gone from his voice. He looked above Elliot's head, apparently staring at something in the distance. 'The watchers want to have control. They want people to fear them, to do what they're told, to know who's in charge. They want people to know who has power over them. And do you know why they want to do that, Elliot?'

This time Elliot didn't. Even if he did know, he thought, it wouldn't be clever to be too clever. Particularly not with the note of fervour that had crept into Richard's voice.

Richard jumped off the wall and came up to him as he'd done before. He was so close that Elliot saw the individual pores in his skin and a patch he'd missed shaving. He gripped Elliot's shoulders, his fingers digging in, almost painful. His eyes bored. Elliot couldn't move. Couldn't look away. Couldn't blink. Richard spoke in a fierce whisper. 'The point is this. It's what Orwell wrote in the book. The point of control is *to control*. The point of having power is *to have power*. The point of using terror is *to use terror*. It's as simple as that.

'Do you understand, Elliot? The power the Guardians have isn't a means to an end. Only the no-brainers, the thickies, the dumbos, the neanderthals, think that. The poor, sad little losers.'

He held Elliot for a few seconds longer, then straightened up and looked away. 'Power *is* the end, Elliot. If you really want it, and want to keep it, you'll remember that. And if you do that, and understand it, you'll discover just how much fun power can be.' He looked down and laughed at Elliot's face, at his expression of confused half-understanding and alarm.

'Get lost, Elliot. We'll be in touch. You can count on that.'

Chapter
9

On Saturday morning Elliot woke early and couldn't get back to sleep. Richard's words still echoed inside his head: *We'll be in touch. You can count on that.*

He didn't want to hear, but nothing, not even full volume on the headphones, blotted it out. Why couldn't they say what they wanted from him?

As if that wasn't enough to cope with, his parents had rowed – or rather his mum had shouted and cried – practically the whole of Friday evening. Nothing in particular had caused it; it was over all the usual stuff: why didn't his father *do something, get up, get out, get off that chair.* But this time, once she'd started she seemed unable to stop until she was physically drained and her anger collapsed into tired weeping. It had begun at dinner and there had been no opportunity for Elliot to escape.

He wanted to talk to her. Not about his own problems – how could she help with those? – not about anything in particular, even. He just wanted to talk to her, and her to talk to him, like it had been back at the flat. But he couldn't find the words any more and it seemed as if she couldn't – or didn't want to – either. It was as if the two of them had less and less to share, their lives separate railway tracks running away from each other into the distance.

And on top of everything, cold and accusing, was the memory of the lie in the changing room. It had come out so horribly easily and been believed so readily, but there had been nothing else he could do. It was hardly as if he'd hurt anyone – in fact he'd done the raw-nosed boy a favour, since no one would be seeking revenge for having detention. All those things were true, yet he felt nothing but rottenness inside.

If only it hadn't been passed on. If nothing had been reported, or if nothing had been said, then the summons might never have come. If . . . If . . . If . . . His thoughts ate away at him like poison, making it impossible to focus on anything else. He picked up a book he was part-way through and dropped it after half a page, the text a meaningless jumble of shapes. He looked at the clock-radio: 06:01. He'd go mad if he stayed in bed much longer.

He threw off the duvet and dressed quickly. Five minutes later he was out of the house, towel and swimming trunks in a carrier bag under his arm.

Shortly after they'd moved to the flat, he'd started to get up early every Saturday and Sunday and walk the half-mile to the local swimming pool. He'd swum lengths, trying to increase his distance and speed every visit, as he'd done back at the leisure centre. Frequently he was the only one there that early. At most there were a few keen types, who ignored him as he ignored them. Knowing that he'd be left alone had been one of the best parts of it.

Something happened to Elliot when he was swimming.

It gave him the ability to lose himself. Pulling up and down a lane, his limbs and body working with quiet, powerful efficiency, smooth and co-ordinated, his head emptied of everything except the stroke . . . the next stroke . . . the next stroke . . . Getting the curve of his arm right, cupping his hand so it bit into the water. Sensing the power of a good stroke – how it drew together all the muscles in his body, concentrated them in a single motion. And when it all came exactly, beautifully right it was effortless, and he cut through the water hardly aware of the weight of his body, not seeking to master it but working with it, letting it hold him. Trusting it. Trusting himself.

It became a place of escape, somewhere he was allowed to forget the ugliness that existed outside.

Since they'd moved to Holminster the only swimming he did was with the team, and it wasn't the same. Then he was swimming for someone else: listening out for the coach's instructions, thinking about how he fitted into the team, how to work together in a competition. There was never a chance for him to empty his mind and be alone.

The pool was all but empty, just one swimmer ploughing steadily up and down a lane. Elliot dived into the deep end, the water smashing up into his face, driving the rubber edges of the goggles painfully into his skin. He sank almost to the bottom and rose slowly, already halfway up the pool. He settled into a front crawl, pacing himself to avoid cramp.

He completed one length, then another. Up . . . down.

Up . . . down. Breathing easily, his body liquid, flowing. He was hazily aware of the swimmer in the next lane keeping pace with him, but otherwise his mind was clear, thinking about nothing but the stroke . . . the next stroke . . . the next stroke. The outside world slipping away . . .

Up . . . down. Fifty-seven . . . fifty-eight. Up . . . down. Letting go of everything else, until there was nothing except the water and his body – and they were limitless . . .

Eighty-nine . . . He could have gone on for ever, but near the end of the length he looked up and the overhead clock showed 7.55, and he knew there would soon be more people arriving, crowding the lanes. It wouldn't be the same then.

He came to the end of the length and stood up in the shallow end. He felt tired but good: worked out, faintly glowing. He peeled off his goggles and stood for a moment, keeping the feeling.

The other swimmer finished his length and stopped too, pulling himself up using the bar. He shook his head to throw off water, then pulled off his goggles and glanced at Elliot.

Their eyes met.

The water suddenly felt very cold.

It was the small kid from the punishment in the toilet block. Unmistakable. Over the past few weeks, his face had occupied Elliot's dreams often enough.

They stared at each other. Then, with a convulsive effort, the other boy scrambled over the edge of the pool and darted into the changing rooms, out of sight.

Of all the people to meet! With a sense of unreasoned urgency, Elliot got out and hurried after him. When he got to the changing room the other boy was struggling with a locker, fighting to make the key turn. He saw Elliot and dropped the key. He backed against the wall, frantically looking to each side, looking anywhere except at Elliot.

It was like watching a cornered animal, Elliot thought – a defenceless creature hopelessly searching for a way of escape. The other boy was shaking, his whole body trembling violently, his thin chest heaving. There were little sounds as he inhaled and exhaled.

Realisation struck: *He's terrified of me. He probably thinks I'm going to attack him.* Elliot felt sick. All the good feeling from the swim had gone.

He took a step back and said quietly, 'Look, I'm not going to do anything, OK?'

His words had no effect. If anything, the other boy looked more terrified.

So this is what it means to have power, thought Elliot. *To stand over someone and have them physically tremble in my presence.* But he didn't feel powerful. There was something awful about the scene. He wanted to step away, get dressed, and get out, but he couldn't do it. He knew why. *I'm guilty. I watched, along with everybody else.*

He bent down and picked up the key. He held it out. 'Here.' Like a peace offering.

The boy's eyes flicked from the key to the lockers, then to the space behind Elliot, then back to the key. But he made no move to take it.

'I'm not going to do anything.'

Still the boy didn't move; stayed pressed against the wall, his chest rising and falling.

Elliot's trunks were clammy and disgusting. The warmth of the swim had leaked out of him. He wanted a hot shower. He wanted to be out of here. He checked the number on the key tag, then looked along and found the corresponding locker. The key turned easily in the lock and the door swung open.

'I'm not going to do anything,' he repeated.

Still there was no response. Elliot felt a rush of irritation. 'Suit yourself.' He opened his own locker, found shower gel and shampoo, and went over to the showers.

It was difficult to lather his hair. His hands were shaking. He still felt sick. Part of it was shock – shock that he could have that effect on anyone – and then self-disgust, revulsion at himself. But that wasn't all of it. Not if he admitted it to himself. The truth was that the encounter had been like re-living a memory, except that in the memory the situation was reversed.

He closed his eyes and started to rinse his hair. A picture formed behind his eyelids: a boy backed against a wall, pressing against it as if it might open up and swallow him. It didn't – of course it didn't – but still he prayed that it would, because there was nothing else to do; they had blocked every escape route. And now they came for him . . .

He opened his eyes and deliberately let soapy water trickle into them. The stinging pain drove away every thought except a frenzied desire to relieve it.

The sheet of paper in his locker said simply '4.15'; there

was no indication of who it was from, or what was happening at 4.15, or where it was happening. But then there was only one thing it could mean: he had been summoned again.

Was getting a note in your locker different from having your name on the notice board? He guessed it had to be. So he still hadn't been selected for punishment.

So what the hell do they want with me?

He expected Oliver to be waiting, but at four o'clock there was no sign of him and he went on into the woods alone. The Guardians were waiting as before, perched on the embankment wall. Elliot pulled his bag off his shoulder and stood looking up at them.

Richard spoke. 'You want to learn some more, then.' It was a statement, not a question, and Elliot waited.

'Yes, of course you do. You want to know all about us. You want to know what the Guardians are, why they exist, why they do what they do.'

Again, Cameron and Gareth seemed content to let Richard speak. But both of them stared at Elliot, as if watching for him to make a wrong move.

Richard looked into the trees.

'We go – the Guardians go – way back. Almost to when this school was founded, in 1876. It means we've got history; we're not just a name taken out of thin air. In different times different people are called the Guardians, but really they're the same. Continuity – that's important to remember. People come and go but the Guardians are always here. Even if today we don't receive the recognition we deserve . . .'

Unexpectedly, Gareth took up the narrative, still staring at Elliot. 'Continuity, Elliot. Remember it. Think what our name means. Guardians: guards, protectors, custodians. What do Guardians do? They defend. They block. They resist. They keep things in their place. That's what we do: we keep people in their place. If they forget their place we remind them of it, and if they try to leave it . . .' Gareth didn't need to finish the sentence.

'The Guardians exist by keeping everyone else in their place. *Continuity*. Remember that, Elliot – because it's how we survive.'

As if on cue, Cameron cut in; this was clearly a rehearsed performance.

'The old Guardians kept a book, a sort of combined diary and record of everything they did, everything they were: names of Guardians, names of people to be punished, names of punishers, details of the punishments. There's some great stuff in there – pretty vicious, pretty bloody. Broken ribs, broken noses, fencing scars – they used to organise fencing duels with the safety buttons off. Messy. But they never let it get out of hand. Everything was controlled, everything was predictable. They knew their stuff in those days. You can learn a lot from them.'

There was a brief silence. Then Richard resumed talking.

'That was when Holminster High was a grammar school, of course. And then they turned it into a comprehensive, and all that stuff vanished as if it had never been. On the surface, that is. No prefects, no form managers, no head boy; the old pecking order, the old hierarchies – all gone.' Richard looked down and smiled at Elliot. 'Am I boring you?'

Elliot shook his head, maintaining his expression of casual – although not *too* casual – interest. He wondered what the point of this was. It was amazing – not to say creepy – that the Guardians could have existed for so long; but he couldn't see why they wanted him to know it.

'It was all quiet until ten years ago, when there started being new entries in the diary after a gap of more than twenty years. There's no record of why we – why the Guardians – re-surfaced, but we were back. And now it's as though we never went away.' Richard looked at the other two Guardians and though nothing was said, Elliot had the impression that an agreement had been reached. 'Which brings me to the point of this meeting.

'From September, we've each got a year left in this place. And when we leave, we need people to step into the positions we vacate. People who share our values, our beliefs. We need *successors*.'

A cold worm crawled into Elliot's head.

This can't *be why I've been called out here. No way.*

'Not just anybody. People we can train. People willing to be educated.'

No way.

It was still half like a game. Richard's voice was gentle, bantering, as if he and Elliot were pretend-playing. It made it worse. If he had displayed emotion, raised his voice, what he was saying would sound ridiculous. But the way he spoke, so deliberately casual . . . Elliot had no doubt that if he put a foot wrong – like revealing this con-versation to anyone – the Guardians would annihilate him, and do so with no more effort than stamping on a chick that had fallen out of its nest. He shuddered at the image that came into his mind.

'So, Elliot. Now you know us. And we already know *you*. We know you aren't one of the crowd. We know you aren't interested in simply being a spectator. We probably know you better than you know yourself.' Richard paused. 'You're already halfway to being one of us. We're offering you the opportunity to travel the rest of that way.'

The unspoken question drove the breath out of him. He wanted to turn and run, but his legs were rigid.

'I should add', said Richard, 'that this isn't usual. It's general practice that only year-elevens are given the chance. But this year, although there are plenty who would *like* to be Guardians – as always – there are few who are truly suited to the . . . responsibility. We have two candidates, but finding the third was becoming a problem. Until you came along.'

The three of them looked down on Elliot. Three who must have each been chosen as they were now choosing *him*. All three of them chosen because they were *noticed like him*.

But they've got it wrong. I'm not like them. I'm nothing like them. Please, let me wake up from this now.

Cameron spoke. 'Most people would feel privileged to be given this opportunity. Do you feel privileged, Elliot?'

Elliot didn't trust himself to speak. Didn't trust himself to breathe.

Richard answered for him. 'No, of course Elliot doesn't believe he's privileged. And why is that?' It was another non-question. 'It's because Elliot knows it's his *right* to be here. He was born for this. He doesn't need to be grateful to us; he doesn't need to be grateful to *anyone.*'

Abruptly he jumped down from the wall. Elliot thought he was going to come up to him as he'd done before. He held his breath, fighting the tremor that threatened to seize him. His pulse banged inside his skull.

But this time Richard held his distance. 'My God, Elliot, look at you! Not a flicker. You've got it made. You're going to *rule* this place when we're gone.'

Elliot's breath escaped between his teeth. His shirt was wet on his back. His stomach knotted and unknotted.

Richard held out his left hand, palm down. As if on cue, Cameron and Gareth jumped off the wall and joined him, each putting their left hand on top of his.

Now they were waiting for *him.*

He could run. He could say *No*. It was *his* choice.

Space and time were motionless. Nothing existed except the four of them, here, in this clearing.

My choice. Except that it wasn't a choice. Not properly. Not when you remembered the changing room, or the toilet block, or any of it. When you thought about those, it wasn't a choice at all.

He watched his left hand come up and place itself on top of Gareth's. He watched Richard bring up his right hand and cover it. Felt the pressure of it. Cold skin on cold skin. He felt himself stepping outside everything; he felt as if everything was happening without him being there. *This isn't real. It's a dream. I'm going to wake up and it will all have been a dream.*

And then the world switched back on. He was real, *there*

84

in the wood, in the clearing, and it was *his* hand, it was really *him*, it was all real.

Richard pressed his hand down. 'Welcome, Elliot. Welcome, Guardian.'

Chapter
10

Welcome, Guardian.

I'm a Guardian.

No. No way. This isn't happening.

This is happening. This is real.

Let me wake up. Please.

You're already awake.

He was to meet the Guardians twice a week for 'training' – what this involved he had yet to find out. If he needed to contact them at any other time, he had to pass a message through Oliver. The Oliver who now avoided Elliot's eyes, and spoke to him without any trace of the self-confidence and superiority he'd displayed before. Who treated him with respect.

Otherwise life went on as usual. The Guardians' identities were closely guarded; only a few trusted Watchers, such as Oliver, ever saw them or knew them by name. To all but those select few, Elliot was simply Elliot Sutton, average year-nine male, member of the school swimming team. No questions asked, no notice taken.

It gave Elliot an uncomfortable feeling of mingled triumph and unhappiness. He'd done it: he'd made himself fit in, made himself noticed in the right way. But in the process something terrible had happened – something he'd never asked for, didn't want, couldn't bear, but that also, in a horrible way, just about guaranteed his safety.

My God, Elliot, look at you . . . You're going to rule this place when we're gone.

He didn't want to rule. *I just want to survive.*

The point of control is to control. The point of having power is to have power. The point of using terror is to use terror.

I don't want to. I can't. I'm not like that.

You'll get used to it, the little voice whispered.

On Saturday morning he woke early from a nightmare. The house was quiet around him. Again he felt the desperate urge to get some space, to get away from everything, and there was only one way he knew how.

This time he took the small canister of film with him. Not that he seriously expected the boy from last week to return. *I know I wouldn't.* But he didn't want to miss any chance of getting rid of it.

You should have just thrown it away, the voice whispered.

A few times during the week he'd come close to doing just that. But each time he'd stopped, remembering the time – a long time ago – when a roll of film from a family holiday had been ruined by the chemist and his mum had burst into tears.

He had no idea what was on this film, but whatever it was, he couldn't just let it be destroyed.

The swimming pool was deserted when he first arrived. After he'd swum a couple of lengths, someone else slipped in from the shallow end and began to lap on the opposite side of the pool. It could have been anybody – at that distance, through the water, everyone was an anonymous body – but he had the strange conviction that it was the boy from last week.

They matched each other for seventy lengths – whoever it was, they were in good shape, Elliot thought. He felt his black mood lifting. Impossible for it not to, in the water like this. Beautiful. No pressure. The world exiled.

It took Elliot a moment to realise the other swimmer had gone. Panicking, he put on a burst of speed to the end of the pool and clambered out after him.

When he got in the changing room, he saw that he'd guessed right: the same small, fragile figure was pulling a bag out of a locker. He glanced nervously at Elliot, but this time made no move away from him.

Elliot went to his own locker and took out the small black canister. He had a moment of doubt and panic. He was only assuming this boy had dropped the film; it might have nothing to do with him at all. *You'll look a right prat then, if you give it back, won't you? Some sort of weirdo who hands out stuff to total strangers.*

He almost put the film back in the locker.

But he didn't want to carry it around for ever. *And I can't just throw it away.*

He called over. 'Hey!'

The figure jerked, as if receiving an electric shock.

'This yours?' said Elliot, holding up the canister.

The other boy said nothing, hunched his shoulders, appeared to shrink into himself.

'This yours?' said Elliot again, although he knew the boy had heard him the first time.

First and only rule of engagement, he thought. *Don't look, don't answer, don't move. Then there's just a chance they won't be bothered to carry on. Not much chance, but a chance.* Answering was fatal. Then they had you. *If you answer, you've helped them notice you.*

He imagined what the boy was thinking. *Answer 'Yes, it's mine,' it gets destroyed in front of you. 'Oh, sorry, Elliot, my foot slipped.' Answer 'No, it's not mine,' it also gets destroyed in front of you. 'Not yours, Elliot? Well, you won't care what happens to it, will you?'*

Elliot went up to him, feeling dangerously exposed, even though it was only the two of them in the changing room, and placed the canister in the open locker. Before he could stop himself, he said, 'I'm not going to touch you. I found it, that's all. I'm just giving it to you. Nothing funny. OK?'

Liar. If he'd just 'found it' – if he hadn't been there, hadn't watched, hadn't *seen,* hadn't . . . *If I just 'found it', how would I know who it belonged to?*

But this time the boy nodded – very cautiously, a small nervous movement, as if he was terrified of upsetting some dangerous animal.

The voice said, *Fine. You've satisfied your guilt. Now leave it.*

Elliot showered slowly, dressed and went out into the early morning sunshine, thinking about what he should have said. *Hey, I'm not . . . I'm not . . . not . . .*

What? What would you have said?

He nearly walked into the other boy; he was waiting on the pavement.

They both flinched.

Elliot hesitated. He knew he should ignore the other boy and walk on past. But another part of him wanted to say, *Hey, I'm not like you think; I'm not like anyone in this place thinks. Don't make the mistake of thinking you know me from what you see.* Which would be stupid, pathetic, dangerous. Which he couldn't ever say.

The other boy fumbled in his pocket, took out the film.

'I'd been looking everywhere for this. I thought I'd lost it. I mean – thanks. I mean – most people, they wouldn't have – they'd have just chucked it away.' The words stumbled over each other. 'It's my competition entry. I thought I wasn't going to be able to enter, or I'd have to take them all over again, and I mean –' He stopped. 'How'd you know they were mine? I mean, I haven't seen you in photography club –' He stopped again and went red. 'Sorry, I didn't mean – I wasn't – I mean, it doesn't matter or anything. I just wanted to let you know . . .'

Elliot was embarrassed by the display of gratitude. He said, uncomfortably, 'Thought it might be important, that's all.' He looked anxiously around. He didn't want to be seen like this, talking to a kid not only from a year below, but also on the Guardians' hit list. Fortunately, early on a Saturday this part of town was practically deserted.

'It's all right,' the other boy said nervously, but as if to reassure Elliot. 'There won't be anyone around. There never is. Never has been, I mean. I mean, I've never seen –' He tried to smooth his tangled hair with his hands. 'I should have had a shower. I was in a hurry. I didn't know who you

90

were. I mean – I'm Ben –' He broke off as abruptly as he'd started.

He was like a scared rabbit, jumping all over the place. Elliot looked around again. Being in the open like this was dangerous, whatever. He said, hoping – what did he say his name was? – Ben would take the hint, 'Well, I'd better be going.'

'D'you want to see the photos?'

Elliot stared at him. 'What?'

'See the photos.' The words flooded out as if Ben couldn't stop them. 'You can come back and see the photos if you want. To my house, I mean. It won't take long to develop them. I've got my own darkroom. Only if you wanted, I mean . . .'

It was as if they were at primary school: *You wanna play computer games? You wanna see my hamster?*

No. No way. This was precisely the sort of kid he did *not* want to be associated with. Some scared midget desperate to find someone who wasn't going to beat up on him.

'Only if you want to.'

As abruptly as Ben had switched from dumb silence to verbal diarrhoea, Elliot's brain shifted tracks. He thought about what else he had to do. He was in no hurry to get back home – not with his parents in the house together. The alternative was hanging around the shops on his own all morning, as he usually did. And although this kid, Ben, was one of the last people on earth he could afford to be seen with, at the moment there was no one around; and if they went back to his house, nobody was going to see them . . .

Get yourself out of here.

Ben lived in the upper end of town – the expensive end. Where the lower end had estates of mean, equally-spaced brick boxes, each with their identical postage stamp of lawn, here it was all grand, sprawling Victorian suburbs, the houses half-concealed behind walls and bare trees and jungles of greenery.

Elliot nervously looked at the upper storeys, imagining people hidden behind the bay windows, watching him without him seeing them. For all he knew, dozens of Holminster High kids lived down here. He could be recognised. Several times he was about to make an excuse to get away, but each time, at the thought of the alternatives, and the likely pleading from Ben that would result, he closed his mouth.

Ben lived in a road called Regency Avenue. Elliot estimated that you could fit three of the houses from Lawnacre Drive into his house and still have room left over. The hallway was at least half as big as the lounge at home. It had framed watercolour landscapes on the walls, polished tiles and a grandfather clock that ticked with a slow, heavy *tock*.

The richness of it all unnerved him. And this was only the hall. *The money that must be in this place . . .*

Ben's mum hurried through from the back of the house, wiping floury fingers on a tea-towel. In an ankle-length dress and with long, red-brown hair held up in a coil with metal pins, she had an almost old-fashioned look, although her face was no older than that of Elliot's mum.

She bore down on Ben, who ducked away from the kiss she planted on top of his head, then turned to Elliot.

'It's so *wonderful* to meet you.' He had the impression she had to restrain herself from hugging him. Why on earth was it wonderful to meet him? She didn't even know who he was.

'And what's your name? What should I call you?'

What should I call you? 'Er . . . I'm Elliot.'

'Wonderful. Oh, that's wonderful. It's so nice that Ben's brought a friend home at last. I was beginning to think –' She cut herself short. 'I was starting to think Ben must be embarrassed by me.'

She laughed to reassure Elliot she was joking. He laughed politely, wondering if she knew the most likely reason why Ben didn't bring friends over. *It's difficult to bring friends home when you don't have any.*

Upstairs, a carpeted corridor stretched away for miles. Ben paused with his hand on the first door off it. He said flatly, 'She knows, if that's what you're wondering.' Now he was in his home territory, he seemed subtly different: older, less jumpy. 'She's convinced herself that having no friends is a phase that people grow out. I haven't worked out if she means me or the other people.'

'Maybe both,' said Elliot. He wasn't sure if he meant it to be funny but Ben laughed, and he joined in. Then he felt sick. A few minutes ago he'd been playing the role of the polite guest to Ben's mother; right now he was sharing a not-really-funny private joke with Ben, like they were good friends laughing together; and yet a few weeks ago he'd stood and watched the same person get humiliated. And worse, he knew that he might easily have to do the same again. *Welcome, Guardian.* He was the *enemy*.

Which of the roles he was playing was real? Were any of them real? How were you supposed to tell?

Ben pushed open the door.

Elliot saw photographs. Everywhere.

Every surface of Ben's bedroom – the walls, the ceiling, the back of the door – was covered in photographs. A few were colour, most were black-and-white. They overlapped one another, jostling for space, one picture spilling into a dozen others, so that from where Elliot stood the whole room was a single work of art – a huge 3D canvas charged with a million shades of black and white and grey. The occasional patch of colour served only to make its absence everywhere else more intense.

Intense – that was the word. It drew him in. He couldn't resist. Up close, he could see properly that each part of the whole was an image in itself, and that each image had been positioned in relation to others so that although they were separate there was also a continuous flow of lines and shapes and shadows. He was awestruck that anybody could have the skill and the imagination to put the whole thing together.

He studied some of the individual pictures. Every conceivable subject had to be there: bleak, monochrome landscapes, white mist boiling off textured greys. A car hubcap, with the upside-down image of a church spire captured in its polished, dented chrome. A house halfway through demolition, one side ripped away to reveal the rooms inside, complete with chairs and beds and plumbing. Ordinary things, but captured in ways that gave them existence and meanings that were unfamiliar and wonderful yet at the same time solid and real.

Eventually Elliot was able to look around at Ben, who was still in the doorway, wearing a peculiar expression: a mixture of pride, pleading and . . . something else.

Ben came into the room. 'What d'you think?' His voice was casual.

Elliot turned back and looked around again, his eyes drawn everywhere. 'I think . . . I think, *wow!'*

Ben said nothing.

'Did you take all these yourself?' Elliot could hardly believe it. The photos were too good. Fantastic. Like something out of a magazine or an art gallery. He said, 'There aren't many colour ones. Don't you like colour?'

Ben threw himself on his bed and lay on his back. For a moment he stayed quiet. Then he lifted his head. 'I like black and white.' The way he said it, Elliot didn't press him further.

There was a silence, but not an uncomfortable one.

Ben said abruptly, 'So what do you do?'

'What, you mean like being a top photographer?'

'Yeah.'

'Oh – you know. I read a bit.' He felt safe saying it to Ben. 'And I swim. That's about it.'

Ben said, 'I like swimming too. I mean, I don't just *like* it. It was why – even when you – I mean, I *have* to go. It's the only place I can –' He didn't finish the sentence.

But Elliot knew what he'd been about to say. *It's the only place I can escape.*

Join the club, he thought.

He noticed a framed photograph on the desk opposite the bed. It showed the head and shoulders of a man, perhaps in his forties, in uniform. He wore a peaked hat with silver braid on the front. His face was confident and authoritative, commanding. He looked nothing like Ben.

'Is this your dad?'

There was a short silence. 'Yeah.'

'He in the RAF?'

'Yeah. Was.' Pause. 'He was a pilot.'

'That must be pretty cool.'

There was no answer.

He turned around. Ben was pulling something out from under his bed: a shallow cardboard box. He sifted through it, stood up and held out a pair of dusty red boxing gloves.

'He was so cool that he gave me these for my twelfth birthday.'

The gloves were huge, ridiculously large. Elliot calculated his hands would fit into them twice over and still have room.

Ben traced a line across them, leaving a red streak in the grey dust. 'He boxed for his college – when he was at Oxford. And he went in for lots of fights before he went into the Air Force. Only amateur stuff, but he won lots of cups.' He sounded reluctantly proud, as if he wasn't sure whether he was or not.

He traced another line parallel to the first, drawing with exaggerated precision. 'He wanted me to go in for it. Follow in his footsteps – you know. He said it would make a man of me. When I said I wasn't going to do it, I thought he was going to hit me.'

'So . . .' Elliot hesitated, unsure of his ground. He

looked back at the walls of photographs. 'But he bought you a camera as well, didn't he?'

Ben shook his head slightly. He was staring intently at the gloves. 'That was from my mum. He was . . . pretty mad at her for that. Didn't want me to have it. I heard them arguing about it once. Him saying I was turning into too much of a mummy's boy. That I was growing up to be a cissy, a wimp, not proper man material. All because I didn't want to go and get beaten up by someone wearing a stupid pair of gloves.'

Elliot was uncomfortable. He would never have admitted anything of the nature of what Ben was saying. Particularly not to someone he hardly knew. Stuff like that he kept to himself. Even if someone was willing to listen, it wasn't the sort of thing you made public. No way.

'The gloves were the last thing he gave me,' Ben continued, speaking to himself as much as to Elliot. 'He got killed three months after.'

It took a while for the word to register: *killed*.

'I'm sorry.' The words sounded wrong, trite.

'It's all right. I've got used to it.' Ben turned the gloves over. 'He was hardly ever here anyway. 'Usually one weekend a month. I preferred it that way. We never got on.' Without warning, he hurled the gloves at the wall. They bounced limply off and fell on to the carpet, fat and ridiculous.

'We never got on,' he repeated quietly. He brushed past Elliot, retrieved the gloves, shoved them back into the box, then pushed the box back under the bed. 'I thought I hated him. I used to wish he'd never come back.' He rubbed his arm fiercely across his eyes. 'I had this dream, often, where he was called up to fight in some new war that'd broken out. And it's on the news about him getting shot down. My dad, the hero, dying in action. Dying. Dead. And then he gets killed in a training accident.'

He turned away.

Elliot couldn't think of anything to say. He was shocked, and also ashamed at himself for being embarrassed before. But there was something else, too. He remembered the names he'd called his own father inside the privacy of his mind. The times he'd wished that he could walk in through the door and not hear the TV, not see the top of his father's head against the back of the armchair as he passed the door of the living room.

He'd wished his dad was *dead*. So had Ben. But Ben had got his wish. *What would I do if I got my wish?*

But then, in a way, his wish had already come true – except that it had come true before he'd made it.

There was no comparison between the grimly smiling man in the photograph on Ben's desk and the man with three days' growth of beard staring into the TV screen. Their fathers had been so different.

But they were both dead.

It made a strange sort of connection between them.

His thoughts were interrupted. 'Elliot?' Ben was holding out the roll of film. He said nervously, 'D'you want to help me develop these?'

Elliot spent the rest of the morning learning about exposure times and film grains and contact prints and fixer, and watching images miraculously grow from nothing but blank sheets of paper and trays of headache-inducing chemicals. Most of the time they were in Ben's cramped darkroom, lit only by a dim red bulb. It was the perfect environment for talking and thinking about nothing uncomfortable – just Ben asking him what he thought about this shot and that angle, this tone and that frame – or working in easy silence, where nothing needed to be said.

A few hours ago it had been impossible to imagine being allowed to be anything like this – anything *normal*. Now it was as if what had taken place in the woods was unreal, an age away, not important. It gave him a feeling he didn't fully recognise, but that was full of light and warmth and ease.

It was a good feeling.

Ben finished rinsing the last print from the film, then snapped the light on. After the dull glow of the safe light they'd been working under for the last few hours the overhead bulb was too bright, and Elliot blinked painfully, trying to adjust his vision.

'If you came back next Saturday, I'd have some more photos ready to print,' said Ben.

His words brought Elliot back to reality with a start. *Next Saturday. Oh my God! What about school on Monday? He's going to expect to be able to hang around with me. How could I have been so stupid?*

Stupid, stupid, stupid, the voice hissed.

'Only if you want to, I mean,' Ben said quickly. 'I didn't mean –'

How do I say it? Elliot thought. *How do I say, 'Look, it's nothing personal, and your photos are amazing, but I don't want you near me at school because you'll destroy the Elliot I've just spent so much effort inventing'?*

'I don't know,' he said awkwardly. 'Not sure what I'll be doing – you know . . .' His mind churned, throwing up ideas of ways to avoid Ben finding him at school. They were a year apart so classes were OK, but anywhere else –

Stupid. Stupid. Stupid.

'I didn't mean any other time,' said Ben. 'I only meant Saturday. I wouldn't expect – I wouldn't expect anyone to risk being seen with me. Not when I'm . . . on the List.'

Elliot felt himself go red. Had his thoughts been that obvious?

Ben looked at the floor. 'I've got used to it,' he said. 'I just want –' He turned and started wiping down the sink, so Elliot couldn't see his face.

Elliot looked at the photographs now hanging to dry.

The silence lengthened.

Chapter
11

Elliot woke with a gasp of terror, his heart threatening to tear free from its moorings, the dream still close and real. He struggled for breath, swallowing air with the desperation of someone drowning.

Gradually, as the darkness faded and he could dimly make out the square of greyness that was the window, he realised he was awake and in bed. Slowly the panic began to leave him, his breathing calmed and his heart relaxed.

It was still minutes before he was able to move. His shorts and T-shirt were soaked and clinging. He pushed back the duvet and clumsily peeled them off, then slumped back. The night air was cool against his hot skin, and he shuddered.

Car headlights briefly lit up the room, and instinctively he looked for the patch of mould. The ceiling was clear, and for a second panic returned, before he remembered he wasn't in the flat.

The dream hovered dangerously near, unready to be sucked back into his unconscious. He had to distract it; he had to fill the empty space of his consciousness, think about something else, to avoid being drawn back in. *Something safe.*

His mind turned over the events of the last few weeks, sifting and sorting, pulling out threads.

He'd imagined that re-inventing himself would involve simply leaving behind the old Elliot and becoming a new one. But the reality had turned out to be far more complicated than that. To start with, it wasn't a question of a single 'old Elliot'. There were at least two: the Elliot he'd been before his dad had been attacked, and the Elliot he'd become afterwards. And nor was there one 'new Elliot'. Every relationship he had to manage – with the Guardians, with Ben, with home – required him to wear a different face, be a different person.

He was splitting into multiple Elliots – Elliots who mustn't meet under any circumstances – and he didn't know how much longer he could handle them, or keep them apart.

He thought of the Elliot he was with Ben: the Elliot who had to be kept secret at all costs. He went over to Ben's house regularly now, every Saturday morning. He didn't know if they counted as friends, or if they were just two people searching for a way of escape who had found it, temporarily, in each other. Sometimes he thought that was what it was most like: a respite from their lives, from Holminster High, but nothing more. Other times, trying to think back to the friends he'd once had – going to the leisure centre or the cinema, hanging out in the park – it was harder to be sure. All he truly knew was that with Ben he felt closest to having something like a normal existence – if anything counted as 'normal' any more.

Usually they spent the morning in the darkroom; Ben was always working on some photographic project or entering a competition. Often they talked: about the photos they were developing, about general photography stuff; about swimming, about nothing in particular. Other times they didn't talk, but that was fine too. Neither of them mentioned Holminster High or the Guardians. It was as if the darkroom and school – and, increasingly, home – were different dimensions of the universe.

Ben kept his word. Between Monday and Friday he didn't try to talk to Elliot, didn't try to make contact. Occasionally Elliot glimpsed him, between lessons or at breaktimes, as Ben scurried – or so it seemed to Elliot – from corner to corner, shadow to shadow, hiding place to hiding place. As if that was going to help him. Nothing helped you if you were on the List.

Different dimensions of the universe. Except that those dimensions were so close to each other, they almost touched. And events in one could spill over into the other.

Like last Saturday. At the swimming pool Elliot hadn't been able to avoid noticing a brown and purple bruise high up on Ben's arm. Then, as they'd walked back, Ben had been on edge more than usual – in a hurry, constantly darting glances in every direction. In the darkroom he prepared the chemicals in silence, his movements jerky and slow, as if he'd never done it before.

Reaching up to an overhead cupboard to get some more paper, Elliot accidentally knocked against him.

'*Aagh!*' Ben dropped the open container of fixer he'd been about to pour into a tray. The chemical flooded everywhere, covering the small worktop, soaking a stack of print paper, dripping on to the floor, filling the cramped space with evil fumes.

Ben stared at the wreckage, one hand clutching his arm, the other hand clenching and unclenching.

'You OK?' said Elliot nervously.

There was no answer.

'Ben?'

Ben looked ready to cry, his eyes unnaturally bright even in the glow of the red light.

'I'll get some newspaper, mop it up,' said Elliot, starting towards the door. He wanted to get out of the confines of the darkroom, away from the choking chemical stench. And he wanted to get away from Ben. If Ben started crying, it would be embarrassing for both of them.

'Leave it.'

Elliot froze. He knew that voice. Brittle. Sharp. Ready to fracture and shatter. Only he'd never heard it from Ben before. He said carefully, 'I thought newspaper might help, that's all.'

'I don't want any help.' Ben scrubbed his arm across his eyes. *'I don't want any help,'* he said again. He wasn't looking at Elliot. *'I don't want any help. All I want is for everyone to leave me alone. If everyone left me alone, I could be just fine.'*

Elliot didn't try to say anything further. He knew Ben was talking about things a million miles away from spilled fixing fluid.

There was a frozen silence in the darkroom.

Ben drew in a deep, shuddering breath. Let it out slowly. 'Sorry,' he said. 'Just babyish.' He rubbed his eyes again.

'Hey,' Elliot said softly. Then he did something he'd

never done before – something that if he thought about it for long enough he'd probably never have done at all. He put out his hand and gently pressed the younger boy's shoulder. As soon as he'd done it, he pulled his hand back, wondering if he'd done the right thing. But he couldn't have done nothing – that would have been worse than doing the wrong thing.

Ben flinched under the touch. Then he said shakily, 'Thanks.'

They'd cleared up the mess. No big deal. But it had shown Elliot how close his different worlds were – how easily they might come into full collision if he wasn't careful, if he forgot which mask he needed to be wearing.

Then there was Elliot the Indifferent: the mask he wore at school and with the Guardians. *Put on the mask. Act the part. Survive.*

That's what it comes down to in the end, he thought. *Acting in order to survive.* He'd been given a part to play, and his survival depended on playing that part to the utmost of his ability. Refusal was not an option, not if he wanted to live.

Before the training, he hadn't thought like that. But he was learning to see the world differently. According to Richard, that was the most important part of his training. Not the details, such as how to recruit Watchers or select punishers and victims – those were important but they didn't come first. They followed naturally from learning to see properly.

His mind went back to a training session two weeks ago, where he'd been alone with Richard.

★

It had been getting late, and the light had darkened. A breeze disturbed the trees at the edge of the clearing.

Richard was talking about what he called 'managing the crowd'. As always in the training sessions, he seemed to be speaking as much to himself as to Elliot, his gaze fixed on a distant point, his voice low and quiet.

'You probably noticed there were no big punishments until after February half-term. It wasn't always that way – at one time they went on all year. But then I noticed something. Immediately after Christmas, most people don't appreciate punishments. They're not in the mood: they're soft and flabby and satisfied with Christmas cheer. They're quite happy to go to them, but . . . no. They take them for granted. Not good.

'So – no big punishments for a whole half-term. At first they don't notice. Then, gradually, they get restless. The little stuff is all very well, but they want action. They want *blood*. By the time half-term is over, they're *baying* for it. Which is just when we give it to them.

'Rule the crowd, Elliot. That's what you must learn to do. Watch it. Understand it. Feed it. But always make sure it's you in control. Don't just give people what they want. Make them wait for it. Make them practically beg for it. Make them *grateful* to you for giving it to them. Never let them take you for granted. Rule the crowd, Elliot. Never let it rule *you* . . .'

Richard broke off. He was quiet for a moment. Then he said, 'What are you going to do when you get out of this place, Elliot?'

Elliot shook his head. It was an event unimaginably far away. 'Haven't thought about it.'

Richard frowned. 'You should. It's important that people like us plan ahead.' He was still looking over Elliot's head to somewhere distant beyond. 'I've got plans. Plans for power. I know it's out there for the taking – for the right person. Holminster has taught me that – the Guardians have taught me that. It's why it's important, for me and for you and for everybody, that they continue to exist.'

Elliot stood and listened, not really understanding.

'Let me tell you what my father does at the end of the day, Elliot. He comes home, he pours himself a whisky, and then he tells me how many feet he's kissed, how many backsides he's smooched, how many times he's – And you know what?' Richard's voice softened, became savagely gentle. 'He likes it. He truly does. That's his idea of the good life.'

He stared at Elliot, and it seemed that he was reaching out across the gulf that separated them. Not in fear, or pain, or anger, but as if recognising and connecting with someone like himself, bestowing on Elliot the recognition of an equal. 'But that isn't for *us,* Elliot. We don't think like that. The Guardians teach us that we're different. Right now, in this place, at this time, there's *nobody* above us. That's why the Guardians exist: to help us learn that it can be that way.'

Elliot wanted to move. His neck ached, and his face was stiff from holding the mask of detached attention that hid the racing of his mind. But he couldn't shift even a fraction; Richard held him as if they were physically joined.

'But don't make the mistake of believing that learning

we're different changes anything. We already *are* who we're learning to be. And we help everyone else to learn what *they* already are. Remember that. Because the Guardians didn't create Holminster, Elliot. *Holminster created the Guardians.* The violence, the punishments, the victims – it's there already. Whatever its name, it exists before us. All the Guardians do is take advantage of it. Remember that. We have power by showing people what they are. We don't force. We don't create. We only reveal what's already there.'

Elliot felt a horrible, vaguely sensed truth coming out of the shadows – a brilliant, cold and merciless enlightenment. And with the light, something inside him that really had died a long time ago, on the cold tiles of a changing room floor, died again. *Why bother to resist it?*

'In *Nineteen Eighty-Four* there's nothing anyone can change – except how they think. Once they learn to accept things as they are, they find it's so much easier. Like everyone at Holminster accepts what we show them to be, because it's so much easier than resisting.

'I want you to attend some punishments. Look at the faces. You'll see it. And once you've seen it . . .'

The crowd behind the pavilion was motionless.

The only noise came from the two boys in the middle of the circle: fist on flesh, bare foot against skin, ragged breaths, little grunts and sighs of pain, of damage caused and taken.

Elliot watched carefully and saw that the fight, although vicious, obeyed rules. There were no hits above the shoulders or around the groin, no headbutts, nothing that might cause serious injury such as a broken bone. At Holminster, violence was always kept within limits. Careful, controlled, regulated.

The crowd, too, watched carefully, following every blow, every stumble, every movement back and forth across the circle. Occasionally Elliot heard a sharp inhalation, quickly stilled. Otherwise, a hush blanketed everything.

The fight was quickly over, with the younger boy lying on the ground. The crowd tensed, hungry, anticipating.

The victor said harshly, 'Get on your knees.'

The loser hurried to obey, keeping his eyes on the floor. 'Now kiss my feet. *Do it.*'

Elliot looked around him. Every face was transfixed, flushed and ugly with excitement, impatient for the kill. What were they thinking? Were they thinking anything?

If it's someone else, at least it isn't me.

He thought that he should have felt some emotion, but all he felt was a dull coldness, an empty, weary acceptance.

Then it was over and the power that held everything together dissolved. The crowd drifted away, until only the loser remained, kneeling barefoot on the grass. He looked up and saw Elliot watching him. If his face registered anything, it was a reflection of Elliot's own state of mind: vacant, tired submission. Without hurrying, he put on his socks and shoes and limped off.

Once you learn to accept things as they are, you find it's so much easier.

Something was changing, Elliot thought. He was learning to push his emotions away, push them deep down where it was hard for them to bother him. His insides were hardening, changing from soft, vulnerable blood and guts to cool, inert plastic. He no longer flinched and shrank away from the world.

But the fear didn't go away. All the time he was conscious of it. Fear just waiting – hoping – to be warmed up. To be given the opportunity to rise. Like it had today.

'Please take a seat, Elliot.' The head sank back into his black leather swivel chair.

Elliot sat uncomfortably on the padded upright chair in front of the desk, the metal edge under the padding cutting into the back of his knees. His hands were clammy. The antique clock on the wall drew out the seconds with a slow, muted *tick*.

The head smiled. He had very smooth features, so smooth it seemed that they couldn't hold any expression other than smiling and not smiling. 'Do you know why I've asked you here today?'

Elliot shook his head. 'No . . . sir.'

The head smiled again, both corners of his mouth lifting a precisely equal distance and not creasing any part of his face.

Elliot swallowed. The air in the office tasted dry and stale. Was the head testing him, probing, hoping he would incriminate himself? He realised he was twisting his hands against each other, and held them still.

'I've been making some enquiries, Elliot. Speaking to your class teachers, asking around, keeping my ears open.'

He braced. *Here it comes.*

'People speak highly of you, Elliot. Actually, they speak extremely highly of you. You're polite, an enthusiastic contributor to school life, you achieve high marks, you mix well socially. Which is why I would be very surprised if you were aware of why I've summoned you. I do apologise for any anxiety I've caused.'

Very cautiously, Elliot's body relaxed. Perhaps this was nothing to do with the Guardians after all. Instinctively he glanced towards the window, where the corner of the pavilion was visible.

'I've called you in here, Elliot, because I believe – and I don't use that word lightly – that you are someone both willing and able to provide an honest and sincere answer to the question I am about to put to you.'

Be careful, hissed the little voice to Elliot. *Be very careful*.

The head switched off his smile. He sat forward and clasped his hands on top of the desk, as if he were about to pray. As Richard had advised, Elliot concentrated on the square of skin between the head's eyes.

The head coughed. 'There are rumours that Holminster school is harbouring what can only be described as . . . a gang. Some form of organised intimidation, if you will, where certain weaker members of the school are being subjected to regular physical abuse. Now, I would hate to imagine – and I do not truly think for a moment – that such a thing could be going on at Holminster. But I am aware that sometimes, regrettably, things can go on in any school that do not immediately come to the notice of members of staff. Which is where you come in, Elliot.'

Elliot focused hard on the patch of skin.

'To the best of your knowledge, is there even one grain of truth in these rumours? No smoke without a fire, if you take my meaning. Has anybody said to you, have you seen anything, that might suggest such activities are taking place. *Anything at all . . . ?'*

All the time the head had been speaking, Elliot had been mentally rehearsing his answer. He looked into the head's eyes and spoke with conviction and with the slightest movement of his head from side to side. 'No.' He let his gaze drop slightly. 'I've never come across anything. Nothing at all like that.'

Don't say anything else. Too many words make you seem nervous.

The head considered him for a moment, then his mouth relaxed and he settled back into his chair. 'Thank you. That's all I needed to know. I really couldn't believe that anything of this sort could have been taking place at Holminster, but I know you will appreciate that I had to be sure.'

Elliot nodded – not too much, just enough to show that he did.

'I'm glad you've settled into life at Holminster so thoroughly, Elliot. It's a tribute to both you and the school.'

It was another five minutes before he was released. He'd had sufficient time to get to the toilet, bolt the cubicle door and kneel over the bowl before he'd thrown up his lunch.

He was wide awake now. He slipped out of bed and put on fresh shorts and T-shirt. He suddenly craved a hot chocolate. Four-in-the-morning comfort – that was what his mum used to call hot chocolate. When his dad had been in hospital, and when he'd first come home, four in the morning was the time both Elliot and his mum often woke, or gave up trying to get to sleep, and came down to the kitchen and waited for the day to begin properly.

They hadn't done that for a long time. Not since the new school.

Not since the Guardians.

He padded downstairs and into the kitchen, and switched on the kettle. It was close to boiling when there was a sound at the door and his mum came into the kitchen. She was dressed ready to go to her early morning cleaning job – it was later than he'd thought.

She stifled a yawn. 'Couldn't sleep?'

'No . . . thought a drink might help.'

'Hot chocolate – that'll do it.' She stopped, about to go out of the door. 'Is everything OK? You look . . . I don't know.'

He had an overpowering urge to tell her. She would be horrified and angry, but at least it would mean that someone else *knew*. But there was no way he could. He wasn't going to be the one who destroyed her hopes of the 'fresh start'. Anyway, there was nothing she could do.

'Elliot? I said, is everything OK?'

He held her eyes, like the accomplished little liar that he was, noticing again how old she looked. 'Everything's fine. Honestly. Go on – you'll be late for work.'

She wasn't satisfied. 'Look, if there's something bothering you and it's something you don't feel you can talk about –' she hesitated – 'body changes or anything like that, you mustn't feel you can't ask me. Promise me that, will you?'

'Mum, I'm absolutely fine. Stop worrying. I'm fine.'

He could see she didn't want to leave it, but, *Thank God,* she looked at her watch and opened the door. Hopefully, by the time she got back she'd have forgotten about it.

The kettle had turned itself off and was gently steaming. He turned off the light and went back upstairs. The thought of hot chocolate made his stomach turn.

Chapter
12

He noticed the girl walking towards him in the corridor only after he'd walked into her and sent the book she was holding crashing to the floor. Instinctively he crouched to retrieve it.

He froze. The book had landed face up. The cover had no picture, just the title and the author's name, both in huge, mock newsprint: *Ninety Eighty-Four. George Orwell.*

'Excuse *me* . . .'

He looked up. He took in the face of a girl: impatient, dark eyes staring fiercely without embarrassment into his, curved down mouth, long black hair that she now tucked back behind one ear with a flick of irritation – and then he became aware of her outstretched hand.

'Sorry.' He stood up and started to give her the book, but couldn't stop himself staring again at the cover. *You should read it,* Richard had said, but Elliot had inwardly recoiled. What Richard had told him about it was enough to convince him he didn't want to know it any better.

'Oh, for goodness' sake!' She snatched it from him. 'It's a *book*, if you're having trouble working it out. You know: lots of little things called *letters* that make up lots of things called *words* that make up lots of things called *sentences* that

115

make up this thing called a *story*.' She rifled angrily through the pages. 'And you've made me lose my place. *And* you've broken the spine. Has it ever occurred to you to look where you're going?'

Her biting voice displaced his shock. He was about to retort, 'How about *you* looking where you're going?' Then she glared at him again, and their eyes met for the second time, and he was silenced. Her eyes were captivating: a beautiful, fierce dark green, so intense they made him think of welling pools of pure colour.

They stared at each other. Without warning her mouth curved up and she giggled. It was like no giggle he'd heard before: not girlish, not childish in the slightest, but bursting with laughter and richness, sounding from deep inside her.

'Listen to me go on!' she said. 'Aren't you going to answer me back?'

He still couldn't speak. Her eyes – which now looked elsewhere – her laughter, her abrupt switch of mood disarmed him. She smoothed the cover on the book. 'Sorry,' she said. 'I didn't mean that: about knowing what a book is. I know you do – know what a book is, that is.'

He had no idea what she was talking about. *Why am I standing here? I should walk away.* But for some reason – maybe the memory of those eyes, that laugh – he didn't move. He said, 'Erm, do I know you?'

Her smile faltered. 'Oh – well, I'm – we're in the same English group. Mrs Davidson. I'm at the front, on the left.'

He couldn't recall seeing her there, but then he had no reason to be concerned where any particular girl might be sitting. In fact, apart from the odd meaningless chat at the bowling alley, girls just weren't an issue for him. The Guardians and their activities were strictly boys only, and he had quite enough to worry about – and too many identities to manage – without getting involved with anything else.

He shook his head. 'Sorry.'

'Doesn't matter.' A vague red darkened her cheeks. Or perhaps he'd imagined it. She tucked her hair back. 'Have you read it, then?'

'Sorry?' He couldn't stop using the word, although he had nothing to apologise for.

'*Ninety Eighty-Four* – I wondered if you'd read it. Because you were looking at it like that – I mean –' Her face was definitely red.

He said, 'Er, no. No, it just looked interesting, that's all. Unusual cover.' *Liar.*

He realised that other than the two of them the corridor was quiet and empty. The last bell had gone and most people had gone home. But still he felt a peculiar reluctance to move, as if some invisible force held him there – held both of them there – and to release its hold he would have to break the spell. He didn't know if he wanted to break it.

'*Hey! What are you kids doing still in here?*'

He jumped. It was one of the caretakers, clearly pleased to be given the opportunity to exercise authority. '*Get out, go on, before I have you reported.*'

They went out into the bright warmth of the afternoon. She made to pack the book away into her bag, then stopped and held it out to him. 'You can borrow it if you're interested. I've already read it a few times.'

The last thing he wanted stuck on his bookshelf was a reminder of the Guardians. He shook his head quickly. 'No – no thanks.'

He said it more bluntly than he'd intended. Her face sagged, and he mentally hit himself for his clumsiness. *Why are you so concerned?* the voice whispered. *You hardly know her.*

He ignored the voice and struggled to make amends. 'It's just that I'm buried in stuff at the moment. I'm still trying to finish *The Mosquito Coast.'* It sounded weak, even with the advantage of being the truth.

Her eyes roved over his face, her forehead faintly creased, her mouth neither smiling nor frowning. It was another sudden change of mood, like her instantaneous transformation from anger to laughter. He wondered which mood she was usually in. The shifts were strangely appealing.

His thoughts disturbed him. He felt oddly breathless and lightheaded. He tried to hold on to the fact that less than five minutes ago she'd been ready to hit him.

Finally she nodded. 'I'll believe you. If you like *Mosquito Coast,* you ought to try *Heart of Darkness* when you've finished. That's by Joseph Conrad, in case you didn't know.' She smiled, taking any edge off her words.

He felt inexplicable relief at having at least partially recovered the situation.

'See you Monday, then,' she said, and turned to leave.

'Er, sure.'

He watched her walk off across the playground and out of the gates, the book in her hand. He still felt odd: uncomfortable, nervous, but also excited. Something had taken place – first in the corridor, then in the playground – and he wasn't sure what it was, if it was going to go further, and if it did, whether it was going to be good or bad.

The feeling lasted all weekend, even when he was swimming, and afterwards, with Ben, setting up a photo-montage for a competition. A few times Ben looked at him oddly, seemed about to say something, then didn't. Elliot was relieved; it was hardly the sort of thing he could say out loud, but neither did he want to have to make up yet another lie.

He wasn't sure if the feeling was a type of fear – or something completely different.

By the following Monday, half of him was convinced she'd have forgotten him and would therefore ignore him. The other half nervously wondered how he should respond if she hadn't forgotten him and sought him out in public.

As it turned out, she neither ignored him nor sought him out. The first lesson was double English, where she acknowledged him with a mildly friendly nod as he came in, but didn't make any move that encouraged him even to attempt an innocuous pleasantry. He glanced back several times as he walked to his desk, but she didn't once look around.

He was relieved, in a way. He had no idea of what he would have said to her. Yet at the same time, he found it hard to concentrate on the lesson. He usually enjoyed English, but for the next hour he tortured himself, im-agining what he would have said to her if she'd given any sign of wanting to talk to him.

The fact that she hadn't spoken to him but was still able to completely occupy his mind simultaneously annoyed, puzzled, alarmed and excited him for the rest of the day. *Why on earth am I interested in what she thinks about me? Why am I even concerned about whether or not she's thinking about me at all?* It wasn't as if he had any burning reason to want to have anything to do with her – or any girl, come to that.

By the end of the afternoon he'd convinced himself that he'd fantasised the whole thing. Nothing had passed between them on Friday. He'd cannoned into her, she'd raged at him, he'd returned her book, and that had been all. Then he spotted her coming out the door to the block of smoked glass that housed the library and computer suite. His stomach kicked, and he hurried across the lawn to intercept her.

'Oh, hi,' she said. Her voice was warm, friendly, but not surprised. Almost, he thought, as if she'd been expecting him to look for her, but had deliberately engineered it so that he would catch up with her *here,* at this precise moment, this exact spot. He was even ready to accuse her of it, but stopped himself in time, realising how crazy he'd sound.

She waited, tucking a stray length of hair behind her ear. Her expression was faintly, but not demandingly, expectant. It was up to him to make the first move: she was giving him the chance, but she wasn't going to help him.

Finally he said, 'You're not the easiest person to find.' As soon as the words came out, he wanted to claw them back. *What a dumb thing to say! Like I'm some smooth-talking movie hard man, and we've just spent the first half of the film playing cat and mouse. You stupid idiot!*

She gently arched her eyebrows and shifted her grip on the small canvas rucksack slung over her shoulder. 'I wasn't aware there was a rule about making myself always available for the attentions of others – "Thou shalt always be around on the off-chance someone might be looking for you" sort of thing.'

He flushed, embarrassed. 'Sorry. Didn't mean it like that.' But she hadn't sounded offended – only dryly amused and faintly mocking.

He struggled for something to say, this time thinking how she was likely to receive and interpret his words. He started talking about *Heart of Darkness*, which he'd begun reading at the weekend, then trailed off, realising he must come across as ridiculous: accosting her, accusing her, and now babbling pointlessly at her. And it occurred to him that if anyone saw him – saw the two of them – it was likely to get back to Richard. Not that it was anything to do with Richard or anyone else. And so what if it did anyway? But still . . .

Her mouth suddenly relaxed into a smile, and she let out that wonderful giggle. 'You look like you're waiting for me to absolve you at confession,' she said, her eyes sparkling wickedly. 'All tense and red and squirmy with embarrassment.'

Warmth rushed into his cheeks, and he felt his face grow redder.

She said, 'I live down Park Avenue, if that's anywhere near your route home. I might allow you to walk part way with me, if you like. By the way, I'm Louise.'

He was conscious of the precise moment he ceased

being confused and alarmed by Louise – by her dramatic and unpredictable mood swings: from animated, upbeat opinions on everything and everyone, through mocking anger, to that wonderful throaty giggle, often all in the space of five minutes – and realised he was in love with her.

He had walked her home that Monday afternoon, and then again two days later. Soon on every schoolday afternoon that he wasn't at Guardian training they ended up walking together to the top of her street. Most times they stopped off in the park to watch the ducks fight over breadcrusts and to talk some more.

He loved to hear her talk. It didn't matter what she talked about: politics, music, art, books. Whatever it was, she knew so much about it, and she spoke so confidently, so effortlessly, so passionately. Sometimes he pictured her as an acrobat: graceful, agile and strong, leaping through space, holding the air, always certain of another bar within reach, never falling. Other times she was a swordswoman: quick, sudden, unpredictable, making razor-tipped lightning thrusts; dancing, feinting, slashing, never conceding ground.

She was everything he wasn't. It was as if he'd been thrown into a new, vibrant, joyful world of experience. When he was with her, listening to her, his breathing quickened, the world moved faster; he was exhilarated, carried away.

Then one day she halted in mid-sentence and looked at him with something close to annoyance. 'Do you have an opinion on *anything*?'

'What do you mean?'

She sighed with exasperation. 'I mean the fact that for two weeks you've sat like a lemon and let me say what I want. I just told you there should be compulsory euthanasia for anyone over sixty – and you agreed! I think I could say anything and you'd still nod. You're as bad as one of those nodding dogs!'

He knew she was right. Occasionally he released a few words, but only when he agreed with what she was saying – which was most of the time – or when she demanded agreement – which was the rest of the time. The problem was that beside her his own thoughts and ideas seemed feeble and insignificant. To open them to her razor judgement would be awful, soul-destroying.

She stopped walking. 'Look at me,' she commanded.

Her face was stern, but softened by puzzlement and sadness. They were close; the road was quiet. His chest tightened. *She's beautiful. I never properly saw that before. I love her eyes, the soft curve of her cheeks. I love everything about her . . .*

She spoke softly, not breaking the moment. 'Tell me. Tell me something about you. Something you love. Don't think about what I'm going to think. Just tell me.'

He could no more refuse her than he could deny the warmth that now flushed his skin. But he couldn't say what he burned to say, because he had no idea of how she felt towards him. He didn't know if she wanted him as more than someone to walk with and talk to; if in saying what he felt he would destroy something precious. So he offered the only other thing he had.

Awkwardly, hesitantly, his heart thudding, he said, 'You know you were talking about when you read? You said how books are like – how they're not just words and paper, but that they're worlds. How when you're reading you're not reading, you're exploring: reaching out, knowing other people, sharing their lives, everything that happens to them. And you said how you forget everything else, forget even yourself; that nothing else matters, and then you close the book and you know something you didn't know before but you can't say what it is.'

It was the longest he'd ever spoken uninterrupted. Louise said nothing, and he knew she was listening with every part of her.

'I think . . .'

He'd used Louise's words to say what he'd never dared admit before. He'd thought of it as a shameful secret: illicit, forbidden thoughts and desires, beautiful and perfect in the privacy of his own mind and body, but not to be spoken of for fear of being told it was wrong and ugly and sinful. And now he had told Louise – but really, it wasn't any longer about books and reading. It was about *her*. It was what he felt when he was with her: how she was a spark of colour in a world of black and white and grey; how when they were together he entered a different world; how happiness filled him until he felt he would explode; and how when they parted, something about him was different, but he didn't know what or how.

'I think . . . that's what I love.'

She still did most of the talking. But now he made an effort, and had the confidence, to do more than passively agree with her. Once or twice he discovered he was talking the way a thought had come to him: excited, animated, ideas slip-sliding over one another, bouncing around. When that happened he became self-conscious and stopped, afraid that he was gabbling nonsense.

Every time he stopped she reproached him, with a mixture of exasperation and sadness. When that happened, he had the urge to throw away every bit of caution – to open up to her, tear off the mask, tell her everything. But he couldn't do it. He still feared that if he did, she might turn her biting tongue – her judgement, her impossible standards – on him, and find him pathetic and inadequate.

Even worse than that, he was terrified that weakness with Louise would make him exposed and vulnerable to anybody else. The Elliots he had invented couldn't just be left to their own devices – they demanded constant monitoring, maintenance, adjustment, refinement. If he didn't pay continual attention, he could, frighteningly easily, say the wrong thing, react inappropriately, get confused as to which one he was supposed to be. If that ever happened – if the paths of the different Elliots ever crossed – if the mask he wore when he was with the Guardians should slip for even a fraction of a moment . . . there would be no mercy. He would be annihilated.

He couldn't do anything that risked that happening. Not even for Louise.

Chapter

13

'Elliot, would you stay behind a moment, please?'

The rest of the English class happily made for the door. He wondered what Mrs Davidson wanted. It couldn't be anything serious: he always handed in good work, and it was always on time, although lately he'd stopped putting in the effort he used to. There was too much else to do and think about: the Guardians, Ben, Louise. Managing and keeping apart all the people he'd become occupied him more and more. In fact he'd left Mrs Davidson's latest essay until the night before it was due to be handed in, and not bothered to check it for mistakes. Not his usual style. He liked to be careful with his writing, go back over it and make sure it said what he wanted it to say.

Mrs Davidson waited until the room was clear, then closed the door firmly and perched herself on the edge of one of the front desks, a row from where he stood.

He played with the zip on his bag, self-conscious and awkward under her gaze. He liked Mrs Davidson, though she'd never singled him out before. She was young, perhaps thirty, and she had an enthusiasm for her subject which set her apart from the other teachers. When she got carried away she paced the room, and when she changed direction her long pony tail swung against her glasses – but no one laughed. He enjoyed English anyway, but with her it was more than simply another subject.

The sun streamed in through the closed windows. He felt exposed, though there was no one visible outside. The noise of a distant lawnmower caused the glass to tremble, and the movement was transmitted to the still air of the room, sending up fat motes of dust that tumbled lazily in the beams of sunlight. Mrs Davidson tapped her nails on the desk, the sound echoing off the unpolished wood. Why didn't she say something? Anything. Was she waiting for him to say something? But what?

She shook her head and laughed. 'OK, you win. I can't stare you out. You're a cool player, Elliot Sutton.'

He waited, uncomfortable, not knowing what she was getting at. He glanced out of the window, then quickly looked back at her.

Her face was friendly. 'I wanted to see you because I'm concerned about the change in the standard of your work. You've always given me superb essays. I like reading them. But recently . . . I don't sense your heart and soul in them any more. I sense someone producing work with less and less effort, and knowing that because they're talented they can get away with it. Please correct me if I'm wrong.'

Because it was from *her,* because he liked her, the accusation hurt him. It was as though he'd let her down, betrayed her trust. He floundered for a reply. 'Er . . . I suppose so. I mean, I didn't –' *Get a grip.* 'I hadn't thought of it like that, but if that's how it looks, I suppose that's how it is.'

Bad answer.

'Hmm.' She gave the impression of trying to penetrate his skin and look through to the real answer she thought was buried there. 'I wondered if you were trying to communicate something through this change in your work. Something more than that you're not bothered about A grades any longer.' She paused, as if selecting her next words with caution. 'I wondered if there were any problems that might be affecting your work. Problems that the school ought to know about, so that we can – if you want – help you with them.

'Elliot? I know everyone goes through a tough time at your age, and that it isn't always easy to talk about problems. And sometimes it's those who have the toughest exterior who have it worst. Those with the most effective masks can find it hard to take them off.'

The shock was almost physical. Elliot had to make an effort not to recoil. She was inside his mind, peering at every thought, lifting off protective covers and going into every hidden place. *How does she know? How could she have found out?*

She smiled. 'Don't look so alarmed. Everyone puts on their own personal armour before they start the day. It's a fact of life. Some people do it better than others, that's all. But sometimes people want help, and the armour prevents them reaching out. And I wouldn't like to think someone was trying to reach out . . . and I didn't notice.'

She doesn't know! His terror subsided and he was weak with relief. *She doesn't know anything. I'm still safe.* And then the voice whispered, *How dare she! She's an English teacher, that's all. Her job is to mark essays and get you through exams, not use cheap psychology to trick you. What the hell is it to do with her what goes on in your life? Stand up for yourself.*

He made his facial muscles relax, adopted the polite blank look that informed someone you had no idea what they were talking about or what they were trying to get at. He shrugged one shoulder. 'I'm fine. Maybe I rushed the last few essays too much. But that's the only problem I can think of. Sorry.'

Her face dropped. 'Oh.'

There was so much in that face and in that 'Oh'. She'd tried to push him, tried to go beyond what she was certain of, and by doing so she'd laid herself wide open. He'd taken advantage of that: told her that she didn't understand a thing, that she didn't know anything. And now she was thinking, and worrying, about what he was going to do: about what was going to get back to the rest of the school.

Hey, you know Mrs Davidson? Only kept me behind because she wanted to know all these 'personal' things, didn't she? Hey, sir, you hear about Mrs Davidson? Is it true she was on her own with this boy and . . . ?

He heard her swallow. From somewhere outside came a faint burst of laughter. He felt disgust at what he'd done, even though it had been defence. She wouldn't try it again in a hurry. She wouldn't act on gut feeling instead of her teacher training. She wouldn't trust herself not to be 'wrong' again. He'd made sure of that.

You shouldn't be so nice, he thought desperately, and wanted to scream at her until she properly understood. *You shouldn't be so nice.*

'Well –' She pushed herself off the desk, walked around to her table and pretended to tidy her papers. She kept her back to him. 'That was all – that was all I needed to know. You can go now.'

I could have made it worse, Elliot thought as he closed the door behind him. *I could have laughed in her face, and made out she was some sort of mad woman. Really and truly, I let her off lightly.*

He didn't feel any better.

He felt a lot worse after the Guardian session that evening.

All the Guardians had been present, but there had been no training. Instead, they'd given him an order. He had two weeks to decide on someone to be a punisher, a punishment, and someone to be punished.

I have to make a selection.

The first two decisions weren't going to be so hard. There were plenty of kids only too willing and able to terrorise someone, and thinking of a punishment was hardly an effort.

It disturbed him that he thought like that. A few months ago the very idea of making such decisions would have been alien and repugnant – and impossible. But as Richard had said, he was beginning to see the world differently, to think differently. He was beginning to see the world as a stage, filled with actors who obeyed his directions, did what he told them. *Their roles are decided in advance, but you have to make sure they keep to them. Put them back in their place if necessary.* It was going to take a lot of getting used to; he wasn't sure he would ever be totally comfortable with it.

But the third decision . . . He felt cold and hot at the same time, a shivery ache running through him. So far, he had watched and learned. He hadn't thought about the reality of being responsible for a selection, *for a punishment*. It was on another level altogether. *He* was going to decide. Someone would suffer because *he* ordered it. How did he live with that?

What does it matter? the voice hissed. *Just choose someone, anyone, and get it over with. What do you care who it is? Remember: if it's someone else, it isn't you.*

And it wouldn't be Ben either. He could at least hold on to that thought. The first thing he was going to do when he became a fully-fledged Guardian was take Ben's name off the List. *I'll have that power.*

But it didn't make him feel good. Somehow the thought of that power – power over life and death – was almost as awful as not having power at all.

Almost.

'You can see it as an initiation rite,' Richard said. 'To be fully one of us you have to prove yourself. You have to prove you have the strength and the authority to organise this and see it through.

'Then we'll truly know who you are – and so will you.'

Who you are?

Which of me is that?

He had started out as one person – the original Elliot, the ordinary boy with a normal life. Then had come the second Elliot: bullied, weak and helpless. And the third Elliot: cool, indifferent, untouchable, Guardian-in-training. Now, to add to these, was the Elliot he was with Ben – and the Elliot he was for Louise.

Which of them was him? Which was the real Elliot?

Maybe I'm all of them.

Mrs Davidson had talked about wearing masks, and that

had been what it was like at first. But you could take off a mask. He wasn't so sure any more that there was a gap between where the real Elliot ended and the Elliot masks started. In fact, he was starting to doubt that between him and the masks there was any difference at all.

On Saturday he swam with Ben as usual. Afterwards, on the pavement outside the swimming pool, Ben said unexpectedly, 'Fancy a walk?'

Elliot hesitated, thinking of who'd be around on Saturday morning, the danger of encountering someone from school.

'We don't have to go into town,' Ben added quickly. 'We can go through the woods. None of the Holminster lot go there on a Saturday.'

Elliot still had the headache he'd woken up with. Perhaps some fresh air would do him good. He said, 'Fine. If you want.'

They cut through the back of a housing estate, on a narrow path boxed in by high, rusty wire fencing. Ben went in front, his swimming bag dangling from one hand, not looking back. Elliot followed more slowly, wishing he hadn't agreed to come.

Abruptly they were in the woods. One moment there was blue sky above, the next moment it was green leaves and branches. The temperature dropped instantly.

Ben waited for him a short distance in. 'See?' he said, as Elliot caught up. 'There's never anyone around here on a Saturday. Except maybe in this weather you get a few people making out – but they don't bother you.'

'Got it,' said Elliot unhappily. Although it was cool, the

sense of leaden oppression remained. The smell of decaying vegetation and tree bark reminded him of why he was usually here. He hadn't realised the woods came so near to the town. How close were they here to the embankment?

He walked behind Ben. Neither of them spoke. He couldn't escape the feeling that Ben was after something more than a walk: he seemed strangely hyper, keyed-up and on edge, but at the same time nothing like the time when he'd dropped the fixer in the darkroom. Elliot had never seen him quite like it. It made him nervous. And whatever Ben said, it was still a massive risk being where anyone might see them together.

I was stupid to agree to this.

Thoughts of the selection slithered into his mind. *How the hell do I choose?* There were seven hundred kids to pick from. Most of them he didn't know and couldn't put names to, and the only ones he both knew and hated enough to select were people he couldn't select – except to be punishers. *How do you select one kid out of seven hundred when not one of them's done anything to deserve being chosen?* Richard had talked about those who deserved it, those that asked for it – the ones who forgot their role, like the raw-nosed kid had, apparently, and needed reminding. But it didn't make it any easier.

The voice whispered. *Make a random selection. It doesn't matter who you choose. Just do it.*

'Hey, look at me, Elliot.'

He was startled out of his thoughts. For a moment the setting didn't register properly. Then it did: the brick wall, the earth bank stretching away either side of it, the open sky.

They were at the embankment.

Ben sat on the wall, his arms outstretched, as though welcoming Elliot into his domain.

The Guardians' wall. The Guardians' domain.

Panic gripped Elliot, crushed his chest. *This is a trap. I've been set up.* Wild ideas churned: Ben was a Guardian; or he was a Watcher; or he'd found out about Elliot and was going to blackmail him.

He spun round, stared into the woods, trying to penetrate the trees. The whole school could be waiting for him. The trees were so dense they could be anywhere.

He'd been so stupid. *Stupid, stupid, stupid.* Should never have taken the risk with Ben. Now he was going to pay. Any moment Richard was going to come out and smile that dreadful smile and say gently, 'You didn't actually believe you'd fooled me, did you? You didn't truly think we wouldn't find out about your past? You didn't seriously believe that *you* were going to become a *Guardian*?'

And then the rest of them: laughing, jeering, moving in on him, until he was surrounded, in the middle of the circle, waiting –

Waiting –

Waiting –

There was noise, deafening him, but he couldn't work out where it came from. Then he realised that it was his own breathing – air foaming and roaring like whitewater in his nose and mouth.

There was no one in the trees.

They were alone in the clearing.

Stupid.

Get a grip.

For God's sake.

Ben was still perched on the wall. 'I always wondered what it was like to sit up here,' he called.

Elliot walked slowly over, his breathing subsiding, his stomach unclenching. Sweat congealed in his armpits. He struggled to find his breath. 'What are you *doing?*'

Ben laughed and spread his arms wider. 'I'm *leaving.* That's what I'm doing. *Leaving.*'

'What are you talking about?'

'I'm leaving. As soon as this term finishes. My mum told me yesterday. We're moving house. Away from Holminster.'

Elliot struggled to take in what Ben was telling him. He said stupidly. 'Why?'

Ben lowered his arms and shrugged, still smiling. Elliot had never seen him smile like that before – without a trace of caution or inhibition, without there being any hint of fear behind it. 'It's like my mum said – there's nothing for either of us in Holminster.'

You can't, Elliot wanted to say. *You can't just leave. I was going to take your name off the List: that was the one good thing I could do. Now I can't even do that.*

He realised he was being monstrously unfair. He had no right to blame Ben for anything.

He tried to appear enthusiastic. 'Great. Way to go.'

Ben grinned again. 'Thanks. I can't believe it. No more Holminster. Like my mum said, we're going to make a new start.'

A new start. The words froze the hairs on Elliot's arms. *Shall I tell you?* he thought. *Shall I tell you how it won't be a new start at all? Not unless you become like me? Would I be doing you a favour by telling you?*

'No more Guardians!' Ben yelled into the woods. '*You hear that? I don't care about you any more. You won't get me now!*' His voice was shockingly loud. The words seemed to hang in the air for ever. Somewhere birds rose noisily, thrashing and squawking.

'*Shut up!*' hissed Elliot in alarm. 'Someone could hear you. Come on, let's get out of here.'

Ben laughed in delight and shook his head. 'I don't need to care any more. I'm out of here.' He started yelling again. '*Good riddance, Holminster –*'

Terrified, Elliot thumped him on the leg. '*Shut up, I said!*'

Ben stared at him, startled into hang–jawed slackness. He reached down and slowly rubbed his leg. 'What did you do that for?'

Elliot tried to control his fear and failed. 'You might be leaving, but I'm not, am I?' He struggled to come to terms with what he'd just done. *I've hit someone before. It's not like I didn't. Kevin Cunningham. He deserved it. Self-defence. But that was then – before. Not now. Not Ben. But – Ben could have wrecked everything. Oh my God! What if anyone was around?* He felt weak and shaky. His hands trembled.

Ben let himself down off the wall. He studied the bag hanging from his wrist, water from his wet towel and swimming trunks dripping through a split and on to his trainers. 'You didn't have to get angry,' he mumbled. 'You only needed to say. You didn't need to hit me.'

Elliot couldn't answer, didn't know what to answer.

Ben flinched.

There was silence between them, but it was nothing like the comfortable silences in the darkroom. It stretched on and on, until it seemed to Elliot it would never end. His head ached. He couldn't think properly. All he knew was that at this moment in time Ben was the cause of his fear: Ben, who had brought him out here, having no idea what he was doing, what danger he was creating for him; Ben, who could have destroyed everything simply because he had no comprehension of who he was dealing with; Ben, who had always been a danger, a constant threat, through his childishness, his hanging on, his clinging.

He saw Ben as Richard might have taught him to. Saw, now, how Ben represented so much the new Elliot didn't want — couldn't afford — to be reminded of. Saw in Ben the figure from the past he'd tried so hard to bury.

He heard Ben say, 'We could keep in contact. You could even visit, if you wanted.'

A danger. A threat.

'Elliot?'

He sucked in the fear and took it deep inside him. He knew now that he was still afraid, and that he was more afraid than he'd ever been. Because before Holminster it had been a dull, stagnant fear: knowledge that nothing was going to change, that the torture was going to go on day after day, week after week, year after year, for ever and ever. But *now* — now it was a savage fear, sharp and merciless. Because everything *had* changed, which meant there was the constant possibility that it might change back — and he knew he wouldn't be able to stand it.

He had to get out of here. 'I've got to go,' he said. 'Got stuff to do.'

Ben looked up. He hesitated. 'I thought you'd be – you know, coming back like usual . . .'

Elliot shook his head, struggling to shake off the noise and images raging inside his skull. 'Can't. Not this week. Maybe next.'

Maybe never. A screaming mask. A mask of screams. He imagined a boot stamping down, cutting off the screaming, destroying, obliterating. *I am strong. I am strong. I can make myself fear nothing.*

Ben was speaking to him again. Asking him. Almost pleading. Like the first time they'd met. 'I mean, I thought –' He looked at his feet. 'I've got a photo I thought you'd – I mean, only if you want to.'

'I said I was busy, didn't I?' Fear made Elliot cruel. *Kill. Obliterate.* 'Which part of that didn't you get? You think I haven't got anything else to do but mess about with that stuff all morning?'

He had to do this. There was no choice. The screaming was still there, but fainter now. He stamped down harder, killing not only the noise, but also the pictures: the kaleidoscope of black and white, the images miraculously appearing on blank sheets of paper under the red glow of the safety light, Ben turning to ask a question, telling him something, the two of them talking –

To stop other people hurting you, you hurt them first. You don't let them affect you any more. You are strong. You do not care. You make yourself so you do not care.

'I can bring the photo to school, if you want,' said Ben. 'Only if you want, that is. I mean, I wasn't – not if you don't. I mean –' His voice ran out.

Elliot's stomach lurched. 'Don't you dare come near me at school. Don't you *dare!*'

Ben stood there, his head bowed, taking everything Elliot gave him. Like a puppy that had been kicked, kicked again, and still came back for more. *The question is, how many times do you have to kick someone before they get the message?*

Ben whispered something. Elliot could hardly make out the words.

'What did you say?' Elliot's voice came out louder, rougher than he'd intended, and Ben flinched again.

'I won't, I said. I'd never do that.'

The sour smell of leaf-rot filled Elliot's nostrils. A dead smell. Decay. Corruption.

Without looking at Elliot, Ben turned away and began to walk back the way they had come. Elliot fought the urge to shout after him.

I should at least have told him, he thought. *I should have at least told him the secret of survival.* Survival wasn't that difficult. It simply meant cutting off all the bits of you that didn't fit. After a while, your new identity became second nature, as if you'd always been like you were now.

The difficult part was managing and keeping apart all the different people you had to become.

He was about to run after Ben, but the voice brought him back to reality. *Don't be stupid.*

He watched the small figure until the woods swallowed him.

He was a risk. Always a risk. You're better off without him.

He realised his hands were shaking. He dug his fingers into his palms.

You are strong.
I am strong.
I have no fear.

Chapter
14

The first two weeks before the deadline passed with mocking haste, days collapsing into each other until all he could do was let himself be swept along to the fate awaiting him. He had to make the selection, there was no escaping it – but as the time sped away, he was no closer to coming to any decision.

All around him he saw kids who would have fitted the requirements perfectly; they stuck out as obviously as if they'd pinned a square of yellow paper to their blazers. Several times he went as far as asking Oliver or the other Watchers for a name and details – their marks, their habits, their friends – and had his intuition confirmed. But each time he held back from a final decision, hoping against hope that he could find a reason to dislike one of them.

He didn't know why it was so hard. It wasn't as if making the choice was going to change anything. *Everything – the violence, the winners, the losers – it's here already. We don't create, we reveal. Holminster created the Guardians, not the other way around.* If he didn't select, somebody else would, and the only thing changed would be that he wouldn't become a Guardian – and then he'd be dead.

He'd never felt so alone. If he could share his misery with someone – if there was someone who would listen and not judge him while he poured out all the foulness inside him – it would be more bearable. But there was no one.

Louise had noticed his preoccupation and wanted to know what was wrong. He invented excuses: too much homework, a swimming gala coming up, nerves about the end-of-term exams. He lived in terror of her discovering the truth, even though it was impossible to imagine how she would ever find out without Elliot actually telling her. School was about the one thing she hardly talked about. It made it easier for him to be a lie to her. He hated being that, when she was so open and honest. But the voice he'd grown to hate, yet depended on for survival, whispered, *Don't feel guilty. Everybody has secrets. What she doesn't know can't hurt her.*

And she hadn't given up pressing him to read *Nineteen Eighty-Four*.

'You ought to read it.'

It was late on Tuesday afternoon. They were sitting on a bench in the park. Elliot threw the last of a sandwich crust out into the pond and watched the ducks dive for it in an explosion of spray and noise.

'Everybody should read it.'

He said, 'I thought you said that forcing people to do things was fascist?' He was learning to be bolder, more confident. Although he could never defeat her when their opinions clashed – and seldom dared try – he had discovered that she relished it when he took her own arguments and used them against her. It was another of her qualities that he loved.

Her face lit up – she was ready to do battle. 'I said that everyone *should* read it, not that they *must* read it. That's a completely different thing.'

'Oh well, if you're going to use clever word play I can't argue.'

She thumped him lightly. 'I'm not. "Must" means you force someone to do something, you give them no option. "Should" means you get a choice as to whether or not to do something – although in this case you're pretty stupid if you don't. In fact, that's the whole point –'

In the space of a few seconds, she'd switched from half-joking to fully earnest. He tried to deflect her, not wanting to talk about it, remembering Richard quoting dreadful lines. *The point of terror is terror. The point of power is power. You will accept it, welcome it, become part of it.*

'You calling me stupid?' He smiled to show he wasn't serious.

But it was too late. 'No.' She bunched up closer to him. 'The point is, the hero of *Nineteen Eighty-Four* is someone who doesn't have a choice. At least that's how it appears. He thinks he *has* to do what he's doing – which is lying about the past, forging history, never saying what he knows to be true.'

He heard Richard again. *Televisions everywhere. Except they're two-way. Everywhere, everything you do, they're watching you.*

'But the point is,' she said urgently, 'he *does* choose. He chooses to disobey the system. He obeys what he believes and risks everything. So he makes himself free . . .'

She was turning the pages in her mind, not looking at him, not looking at anything, talking to herself as much as to him – almost as Richard did, Elliot thought. But if he said nothing he would be dismissing her, throwing water on her fire, and he couldn't bear to do that. He said clumsily, 'So does he win?'

'No.' She frowned sadly, but not at Elliot. 'No. But that's not the point.'

It seemed to Elliot that it had to be completely the point. If you hadn't won, you'd lost. What else was there to say about it?

She provided the answer – if it was an answer – to his unspoken question.

'They beat him in the end. But until they do, he's made himself free. That's the point. He isn't thinking like they want him to think: it's *him* choosing, not them forcing him. And when they win, when they make him think in the way they want, they don't really win at all. Because the only way they can do it is to destroy him.'

His mind filled with further doubts and confusion, and he could think of nothing to say. He wanted to put out his hand and touch her, brush his fingers against the pale red of her cheeks or stroke her hair, press it behind her ear . . .

She shook her head as if waking herself, and looked at her watch. 'Listen to me go on! Hell! I told Mum I'd be back by now – you should have shut me up.' She got up, hesitated, then sat back down. 'I've been meaning to ask you: d'you fancy going to a film on Friday? They've got some really dumb sci-fi picture on at the multiplex, but it looks like it might be bad enough to be funny.'

It was the first time she'd suggested doing anything

more than the after-school walks. Did it mean she wanted them to be more than good friends? Or was it nothing more than that she was keen to see the film? The question of them being officially 'an item' or not had never come up, and he hadn't wanted to be the one to raise it and risk spoiling what they already had. But now Louise had gone a step further.

She got up again. 'It was only an idea.' For the first time since he'd known her she appeared embarrassed. 'Sorry, I know you've got lots on your mind; I shouldn't have mentioned it.'

He was mortified. 'No – please.' He quickly stood up and went to put his hand on her arm, but stopped himself, not sure how she'd react. 'I'd love to go. Definitely. Absolutely. Really.'

'Really? You mean it?' Her expression sent a warm tingle through him and his mouth went dry. She glanced at her watch. 'Look, I've got to go. I'll see you tomorrow.'

As soon as she'd gone, the warmth faded. He watched the ducks, trying to sort out the turmoil that boiled in him.

The way she had talked about *Nineteen Eighty-Four*, it might have been a different book from the one Richard described. Invariably in the training sessions Richard read a passage from it, but what he quoted, the way he talked about it, was nothing to do with freedom, or making choices, or any of that.

Richard had to be right. He was right about everything else. But Louise had explained it so passionately that he had to believe her too, and also he *wanted* to believe her because he loved her. He had a sense that what she'd said was important, and that he should understand it. But what did she mean when she said the hero became free by losing? Or had she even said that?

His head ached. His thoughts tripped over one another in confusion and, perhaps, in spite. He couldn't think any more; he didn't know how he should be thinking or what he should be thinking; and there was no one to talk to, no one to help him. *What does it matter anyway? Nothing I think is going to change anything. So why bother?*

By the time he got home he was tired and fretful, ready to snap at the next person he saw. As usual, the TV was on. He stopped next to the living-room doorway and looked at the top of his father's head, protruding above the back of his armchair.

I wish you were dead. The thought came quickly, shockingly. *If you were dead, I wouldn't have to see you, I wouldn't have to think about you. I could forget you ever existed. I could get on with my life.*

He was shaken by the force of his hatred. It pulsed out of him, black poison spewing into the air, covering everything it touched. How could his dad not sense it? Terrified, he hurried past and upstairs.

In his room he was safe. He just needed some space to breathe, to escape. *That's all. Then I can think properly.* He lay on his bed, his head on fire. He struggled to blank his mind, stared at the ceiling. *White paint. No patterns to follow. No good. No escape.* His eyes hurt, and he squeezed them shut as if that would extinguish the world.

Behind his eyes was a tumult of shapes and stars and swirls of electric colour. He tracked their movement, concentrating, losing himself in them. Gradually the inferno subsided.

Too soon he had to go down for dinner. As usual, the atmosphere at the table was strained. His mother looked tired – he remembered that last night had been an overnight at the nursing home. If there were no problems there she got a few hours' rest before her morning cleaning shift, otherwise she worked right through from early evening to lunchtime the next day. He ought to ask her if she was feeling OK, but he didn't trust himself to speak.

They ate without talking. He wondered if she'd had another row with his dad. He hadn't heard them.

I don't care.

Later he came downstairs again to grab an aspirin for his headache. His mum was sitting at the kitchen table, sipping a mug of tea.

'I forgot to tell you,' she said. 'I've been asked to work an afternoon shift next Wednesday, so can you make sure you're home by five to put the oven on?'

He panicked. Wednesday was a Guardian evening. 'Why can't Dad do it? He's the one who's here all day.'

She said steadily, 'Because I'm asking you to do it. Because you know I can't trust your father to do it. Because I really don't think it's that much to ask – you've told me all you do is hang around with your mates from school, anyway.'

He had tried, a long time ago, to stop her asking awkward questions. But because he was tired and poisonous, he snapped at her. 'What do you know about what I do when you're not around? Maybe I've got more important things to do that you've got no idea about.' He regretted the words even as they came out of his mouth. But it was too late.

'You obnoxious, ungrateful little *monster!*' Her face was white. 'After every effort, after everything I've done to help you, to get you through everything, you give me *this!*'

Stricken, he tried to repair the damage. 'I didn't mean –'

'You meant it exactly. I'm not stupid, you know. Don't think I haven't noticed the looks you give me when you think I'm not watching, or the fact that you won't even take the trouble to tell me about your day, or ask me about mine. I'm not good enough for you now, I can see *that* perfectly.'

'No, you've got it all wrong –'

She slammed the mug down, breaking off the handle, the body of the mug shattering, tea and shards of pottery spilling over the table. 'Don't you *dare!* Don't you *dare* tell me that as if I didn't know it already!'

'I'm not –'

'You think I don't know? I'm the one who's been wrong all along, aren't I? Everything I do turns out wrong. I marry your dad, he ends up crippled by those – those *evil* – those – I mean, I should have seen that coming, shouldn't I? And of course, I was stupid enough to imagine that we could all make a fresh start here, start all over again and make something better of our lives. *Wasn't I?* Oh, yes, I'm always wrong. Wrong, wrong, wrong. That's me.'

Her voice pulverised his brain, reduced it to cold mush. How could he have realised that she felt like that? He'd known the move was supposed to be a new start for all of them, but he hadn't had the faintest inkling of how important it was for *her*.

She didn't talk to me. How was I supposed to know?

There was a long hush and he thought she might have finished. He didn't dare move or look at her. He looked at the table top, at the wreckage of the mug and the ragged streams of pale brown liquid.

'It's not just you that has a life, you know.' Her voice was quieter, but no less awful. 'I'm not just a robot that does the washing and cooks the dinner and handily isn't around the rest of the time. I have stupid, crazy hopes and dreams, that we might end up with something better than this. You know? I have this crazy idea that one day we might be able to get back to something like the life we used to have.'

Abruptly she stood up and went over to the sink. She began unstacking plates from the drying rack. From the living room came the faint fake laughter of a TV audience. All this while, his father hadn't stirred. Had he even heard? Had he even known that anything outside his head had actually taken place?

There was a smash as two dinner plates shattered on the floor.

His mother stood with her back to him, her head bowed over the sink. 'Go away,' she said dully. 'Get out of my sight. I don't think I could stand to look at you again this evening.'

He went up to his bedroom and lay on his back on the bed. There were vague sounds from downstairs. He shut his eyes and concentrated on nothingness. By concentrating very, very hard, he was able to dissolve every sound, every sensation, every thought, every emotion – to imagine he was nothing but cold, empty space, spreading out for ever.

He woke to pitch darkness. The clock radio showed 02:30. He wrapped the duvet more tightly around himself. But now he was awake, he had the urge to pee. Reluctantly he got up and trod over to the door.

He stopped.

Someone was crying. They were doing it very quietly, small, stifled hiccups and sniffs, obviously not wanting to be heard. There was only one person it could be.

He thought back to her anger, only a few hours old. No, there was nothing he could say that might comfort her. She wouldn't want to see him.

He took his hand off the door and crept silently back to bed, his bladder uncomfortably tight. He tried to get back to sleep. The evening flashed in front of him like a badly edited video. The cup, smashing in slow motion, brown tea and blue shards of pottery exploding across the table, only the handle left intact, still in her hand. Where was his dad? The top of his head, black, greasy hair, protruding over the top of the armchair.

He had a horrible urge to start crying himself. Instead, he put on the headphones and turned the volume up high.

Chapter
15

After each of Richard's terse questions, Elliot heard himself respond. It was as if he listened to another person speak.

'Name your punisher.'

'Sean Ashmore.'

'Name your punishment.'

'Fight.'

'Name your selection.'

'Simon Kilworth. Year Eight.'

Simon Kilworth was short and fat, and never to be seen without the big white handkerchief he perpetually sniffed into. He got high marks and was excused from games. The type most kids, if they had to think about it, didn't like – probably including Simon himself, Elliot thought.

'Fight' meant exactly that: good old-fashioned one-on-one violence. Shirts off to avoid damaged or stained clothing – potential incriminating evidence that might get parents involved. Fists only, no hits above the shoulders – black eyes, facial bruises and split lips were all forbidden, not because of any sense of mercy, but for the obvious reason that they showed. It was probably the least humiliating of all the big punishments, which was why

Elliot had chosen it. If Simon was sensible, he'd submit quickly and get it over and done with.

Richard returned his fountain pen to his jacket pocket and closed the leather-bound book used to record Guardian activities. 'Well done. Now all you need to do is inform Oliver, so he can put the name on the notice board. And when it's over, you'll be one of us.'

Elliot felt nothing. He felt nothing most of the time now. The day after the incident in the kitchen he'd gone down to the swimming pool before school, seeking refuge, only to come out after four lengths. In the water, his mind refused to clear. All he'd experienced was a heavy awkwardness in his limbs and the unpleasant sensation of water trickling into his ears. The swimming was pointless: a mechanical movement of body parts, nothing more. It was no longer an escape.

There *was* no escape.

Escape for Louise.

When he was with Louise, and when he thought of her, he did escape. She was the only thing that generated any response, any emotion in him. She was the only thing that hadn't been destroyed or despoiled. Seeing her this evening was going to be his first moment of life in three days.

The meeting over, Gareth and Cameron had gone off home. Elliot was about to do the same, when Richard stepped in front of him. He dropped a hand on Elliot's shoulder, smiling in a way that made Elliot uneasy. 'Hey, enjoy your evening. But promise me you won't get over-ambitious, will you?'

'What are you talking about?'

Richard winked. 'I understand you're entertaining a

lady friend tonight. A romantic evening, just for two. Very nice. I didn't realise you were a hit with the fairer sex too.'

'Who told you about that?' He was dismayed that it was no longer a secret, although it was really no surprise – the Watchers were everywhere. He wanted to keep Louise totally apart from the rest of his life. For some reason he also felt nervous, although the fact that he was going out was none of the Guardians' business.

Richard raised an eyebrow. 'No need to get defensive. News travels fast in this town – as if you didn't know.'

'Yeah, right.' Elliot recovered himself. 'We're just friends, nothing else. Nothing *ambitious,* whatever that's supposed to mean – if that's what Oliver's told you.'

'Whoah there!' Richard held up his hands in mock surrender. 'Oliver would not dream of even *suggesting* anything of the sort. And for my part, I'm quite sure that with your reputation to consider, you've worked out exactly how you're going to play this one. I just had the idea you might be interested in some expert advice from one who knows – if you know what I mean.'

Elliot was cautious, but the uncomfortable truth was that he hadn't worked out anything – notably because he had no idea what he should expect from the evening. Sex education videos always concentrated on the technical stuff; they had nothing to say about the business of going out with a real live person.

'What sort of expert advice? About what?'

Richard put an arm around his shoulders. 'Elliot, Elliot. You must learn to be less defensive. All I'm saying is that there's certain things you need to know if you want to keep a girl happy – if you know what I mean. You don't want her to be the one that dumps you, do ya? Thought not. So listen up close . . .'

The film wasn't as bad as it might have been – although, as Louise pointed out as the closing credits rolled, the computer-animated mutants deserved an Oscar over the human actors any time. And he would have hated it without her being there.

Going out with a girl was a new experience for him. He'd been unsure of what was supposed to happen in terms of who paid, and whether this was supposed to be anything more than the two of them watching a film while sitting next to each other. In the end Louise allowed him to buy her an ice cream, and then halfway into the film her hand made its way into his and remained there until the end. He had stayed very still, nervous of giving a wrong signal.

When they came out of the cinema, she kept hold of his hand. It was still light, the moon visible but a faint yellow crescent. Anxious not to be the one to finish the evening, he said, 'I'll walk you home – if that's OK.'

She pressed his hand. 'I'd like that.'

They walked slowly, but it seemed that no time elapsed before they reached the top of her road. Neither of them had spoken since leaving the cinema. He began to panic. Was she expecting him to say something? What was the right thing to say when they parted? 'Goodnight'? No, too formal. 'Thanks'? No, he needed to say something more.

A few doors away from her house, Louise stopped and faced him. She moved closer, until there was almost no distance between them.

The air was warm and still. The road was empty of people.

She took hold of his other hand. There was a hard knot in his stomach. A warm shiver passed through him.

She said softly, 'Don't I get a goodnight hug, then?'

Her voice, her question, her closeness, dissolved him. He couldn't move. He was weightless – as insubstantial as a pollen cloud, his molecules barely clinging together, suspended in air, gently trembling.

She let go of his hands and put her arms around him. He was crushed against her, her hands pressing him into the warmth and soft curves of her body, his face against her neck. He breathed her, tasted her, drank the subtle, unfamiliar scent of her skin, her hair, all of her.

She pressed him closer, and then her fingers gently scraped the back of his neck. He gasped as soft electricity rippled through him.

His defences were breached. The need for comfort was close to overwhelming. He was ready to confess everything, lay himself wide open to her. He was ready to trust that she would understand and tell him that everything was going to be all right, and let him cry into her shoulder like a small child.

Her hold tightened. She whispered, 'I like you.'

The words made him catch himself. He desperately shoved the thoughts away, shuddering inwardly at how close he'd come to blowing everything. Richard's words from earlier in the evening came back to him. *If she says anything at all like 'I love you', or even 'I like you', that's your signal. That's when she's asking you to take it to the next stage.*

You've got to be ready for it, and as soon as she's said it, you do what she's asking for.

Richard had then given a graphic, step-by-step account of what the next stage entailed.

He had never felt further away from wanting to have sex. All he wanted was to stay in the same position for the next hundred years, to be held like this and never let go. But it was no use. He knew now, from what Richard had said, that through his naïvety and timidity he'd been holding back their relationship. Louise didn't want to hold back — she'd given him the signal. If he didn't respond, the news would be around school the next day as fast as headlice in primary school: *Sutton can't do it. You know, I went out with him and all he wanted to do was hold hands and stuff. You know, I think he didn't know what to do . . .*

Miserably, he let his hand move off her back to where Richard had instructed.

She ripped away from him. His jaw caught painfully against her shoulder, making him bite his lip.

She stared at him. 'What are you doing?'

He said, stung, 'Isn't that what you wanted?'

'No it flipping well isn't!' She took another step back from him, towards the haze of light cast by the nearest street lamp. 'What on earth made you think it was?'

He tasted blood, and wiped the back of his hand against his mouth. He couldn't believe her sudden change. 'You were the one asking for —' The first creeping uncertainty entered his mind. He tried again, but the words sounded weak, as if he didn't believe them himself. 'I thought you wanted me to —'

He looked down at the dark smear on the back of his hand. A confusion of doubts swirled around him. He couldn't have listened to Richard properly. There was no way Richard could be wrong: he'd described it so confidently, so explicitly.

It was his own fault. He hadn't listened. And now he'd wrecked it, shown himself to be a total amateur. By lunchtime on Monday, everyone at Holminster High would know. He was finished.

Louise was probably already working out who she was going to phone when she got back home. There was no point in giving her more ammunition by begging her to keep it a secret. He said wretchedly, 'I'd better be going.'

She looked at the pavement and shook her head slightly. She said quietly, 'All I wanted was – Oh, what's the point. You had to ruin it all, didn't you? You had to turn out to be exactly like every other bloke.'

'I'm sorry,' he said uselessly.

'Yeah, I bet. Sorry you missed out on a good grope, you mean. And now I suppose to make up for it you'll spread the word amongst all your mates that I'm a lesbian, or frigid, or something equally complimentary.'

It took a while for her words to sink in.

She thinks I'm the one who's going to win on this one.

The realisation brought a jolt of shock. With it came the faint hope that, after all, he might have a chance of getting out of the situation intact. He said carefully, 'I'm not going to say anything. That is, I'm not going to say anything if you're not.'

She looked contemptuous. 'Why should I want to tell

the world I was stupid enough to think any bloke would have more than one thing on his mind?'

He felt another jolt. *You stupid prat, Elliot! She wasn't expecting anything like that at all.* And suddenly, to his horror, the whole façade he was trying to maintain, his fake air of calm, his pretend understanding of and control over the situation, dissolved into nothing. He blurted, 'I thought that was what I was supposed to do. I thought that was what was supposed to happen – that's what he said.'

Her anger faded marginally. 'What are you talking about? Who said?' When he didn't answer she said, not angrily, 'Are you really trying to tell me that this is all because you believed what some spotty little schoolboy told you? Someone who's probably never so much as touched a girl in his life? Hot sex tips from the boys behind the bike sheds? I thought you were different from all that, Elliot. That's why I wanted to go out with you.'

Self-pity burned his eyes, threatening the last remnants of his self-control. 'I'm sorry,' he said again, hearing how pathetic the word sounded. There was nothing else he could say; all he wanted now was to get out of her sight before he started blubbing.

As if sensing his state of mind she said nervously, 'I've got to get back.' She ducked away from him, half-running down the pavement, the sound of her heels loud in the stillness.

He didn't wait for her to reach her house, but began walking over to the opposite side of the road.

'Elliot?'

He stopped in the middle of the road and looked back.

Louise had stopped halfway inside her gateway. She was partly hidden in the shadow of the tall hedge either side.

'You did promise you wouldn't say anything about this, didn't you?' she called. Her voice was hopeful, not threatening.

He said, too eager, too loud, 'Yes – I mean, no. I promise. I mean, I won't say anything.' *You're pathetic.*

She didn't move. She expected him to say something – that must be why she was waiting, and he wanted to say something, but his mouth wouldn't form the words properly. Then, as he was turning to leave again, he heard, 'G'night.'

He whirled round but she'd gone. He called out anyway. 'Goodnight.'

By the time he got home, the night air had helped wash out his head. He lay on top of his bed with the light out, and stared into the darkness.

He'd allowed the old Elliot to reassert control. He'd come a heartbeat away from undoing everything. He couldn't afford to let it happen again. He had to kill the old Elliot, once and for all.

You'll never kill me. How could you? I'm part of you. I am you.

He would find a way. He hadn't come this far to let *him* back in control, wrecking everything.

Wreck what? You aren't exactly doing wonderfully without me, are you? If you'd let me speak earlier tonight, none of this would have happened.

She said goodnight, didn't she? She can't have been all that mad.

You were lucky she didn't scream the street down.
But she didn't.
Listen to yourself! You don't believe what you're saying.
I'm not listening to you any more.

He drifted in and out of uneasy unconsciousness, images swimming in and out of vision: Louise tearing apart from him, her face distorted in shock and fear. (Or was it only shock? Had he imagined the fear?) Richard leering, his eyebrows contorting into impossible shapes like some obscene animal, and whispering, 'What you've got to do is *this* . . .' (But Richard couldn't be wrong – it was his own fault, he hadn't listened.) Mrs Davidson shouting, 'Were you trying to *communicate* something? (But how could she have seriously expected him to tell the truth?) Ben, his arms pinned by Kevin Cunningham, his face distorted, screaming at Elliot, *'I'll get you! You could have saved me. You'll wish you never met me –'*

Finally, exhausted, he slept.

16

All weekend he agonised over whether or not to phone Louise. Several times he went as far as dialling her number, then panicked and cut the connection before it rang. In the end he decided that it was better to let her have time to calm down. But he didn't want to leave it too long – the longer he didn't speak to her, the harder it was going to be.

He caught up with her at morning break on Monday, as she was about to go into the library and computer block. She saw him, hesitated, then moved away from the door and turned properly to face him.

'Hi,' he said cautiously, not sure what reaction to expect from her.

'Hey,' she said softly, folding her arms over the folder she carried. Her eyes flickered, catching on Elliot for a moment, then down to the ground, to the side, catching again on him, before coming to rest on the folder in her arms.

Elliot looked around, hoping that no one was watching, wanting no one to intrude. He said nervously, 'About Friday night. I – I don't know why I did that. I was – anyway, what I mean is, I'm really and truly sorry and – I wouldn't blame you for a second if you told me to get lost now, but – I mean . . .'

He couldn't say what he meant. He meant, *Do you still want to see me? Do you still want to talk to me, make me happy, make me amazed with the pictures you paint in my head? Do you still want me to listen to you, talk to you, ask you questions, be stupid, be amusing, annoying? Do you still want me to be anything at all to you? Would you ever consider touching me again as you did on Friday night, your fingers on my neck, on my head, your body close to mine, so close that we might almost have been not two people but one?*

But he didn't know how to put it into words that could be spoken out loud and that Louise might accept. Was she looking for a grovelling apology – for him to get down on his knees and beg forgiveness? It had never been her style before, but this was a whole new situation, and maybe the rules were different.

Or was she looking for him to pretend nothing was changed between them: that nothing had happened that shouldn't have happened; that nothing had happened that had possessed any real significance; that nothing had happened that mattered any more than being something to laugh about and put down to experience; that nothing had happened that couldn't, shouldn't and wouldn't be ignored or forgiven or forgotten?

He looked at her, trying to search her face for any hint of what she was thinking, what she was preparing to say to him.

After what seemed like a year she said, still looking at her folder, 'I'm sorry too. I – I shouldn't have said what I said on Friday. At least, not all of it.'

The last sentence was just a hint of the Louise he knew, the Louise who was sparky and fierce and self-confident, and his stomach flipped slightly.

But then she looked at him properly, and he saw that it still wasn't Louise. It was Louise's eyes and hair and mouth – all the physical characteristics he knew and loved – but the something that made her more than that to him wasn't there.

She breathed out. 'I thought a lot about what I wanted to say, and I don't know if this is going to come out right, but hear me out, OK?' She could have been reading off a script.

'I know you're a boy, and that boys are only ever supposed to be after extended foreplay – I'm hardly unclued up about that sort of thing. And I was hardly thinking you wanted to just talk to me for ever. But you –' either he imagined it or she gave a small shudder – 'you seemed to be this sweet-natured, gentle person; you were almost –' She laughed shakily, embarrassed. 'I thought you were almost *innocent* or something like that. I don't know – I mean, you weren't constantly putting your hands all over me, or eyeing me up, or buying me presents and then – and that night, we were so close, and I didn't know if you were thinking you might kiss me, and I thought that if you weren't – I'd have to kiss you – I mean, I *wanted* you to kiss me – and that –'

She clutched the folder to her defensively. 'That was all I was ready for. That was all *you* made me ready for. And then when you – when you did *that*, it was as if there was suddenly a totally different person there, and it was like – I can't explain properly what it was like, but it was – and I

163

freaked. I mean, I totally did. I didn't know what to expect next. I didn't know what you were going to do. It was like being with Doctor Jekyll and having him turn into Mister Hyde.'

He'd never before seen her so unsure of anything. He was used to her certainty, her highs of anger, sadness, joy, melancholy, her clean, sharp, beautiful emotions. Never as if she didn't know what to think. *Never like me.*

He said, miserably, 'I wasn't going to do anything. I'd never have – not like *that*. Don't you believe me?'

She shook her head. 'Maybe. Probably. Oh, I don't know, do I? I do now, after you've said it, but afterwards I'm going to think about what happened, and then –' She hesitated. 'I was stupid, I was naïve, and I suppose you could accuse me of leading you on. Is that what I was doing? Was that what you were thinking?'

He couldn't believe she was speaking like this. 'I didn't say you were doing anything. I said I was sorry. I meant it. I don't want to accuse you of anything.' He cringed inwardly at the pleading in his voice.

She shook her head again. 'That isn't really what I meant, anyway. I'm not accusing you of being some weirdo but –' She took a deep breath. 'Everything at Holminster is so – so *mean* – so *vicious*, somehow. I hate it. The stupid Guardians – all the boys waiting for those horrible little squares of yellow paper to appear. And the girls aren't much better, with their catty gossip and spitefulness. They're all just *blobs* – you could exchange them tomorrow for a new set and it'd be hard to know the difference. Apart from the geeks. And they're no good – you can't talk to them, at least not about anything that doesn't involve modems or why the theory of relativity was wrong, or why we should all be living on the moon –'

He loved her when she started on like that. He wanted her to keep going, to be like she usually was. But she stopped almost as soon as she'd started.

'I wanted you to be different,' she said. 'I didn't want you to be like everybody else. And I thought you were. And now – I don't know who or what you are any more.'

She stopped, as if the script had come to an end.

I'm whatever kind of person you want me to be, he thought. *Anything at all. Give me the mask and I can wear it.*

She stood there, sorrowful and uncomprehending. The same as that night, he wanted to explain to her – to tell her the truth. But he knew even more surely now that there was no way he could.

When she had mentioned the Guardians, for a moment – the briefest moment – hope had flared inside him. She knew about the Guardians as, he supposed, probably all the girls knew – but she didn't understand even the first thing about them. By calling them 'stupid' and comparing them to girl fights she'd shown that. So even if she found out he was involved, it might not be a disaster. She would be disappointed by the fact that he wasn't as 'different' as she wanted, but she wouldn't necessarily reject him out of hand.

Then, as quickly as it had grown, the hope died. If she didn't know the true nature of the Guardians, he could never tell her about the fear that lay at the heart of him, that was always ready to rise and engulf him. He could never explain to her the choice he was faced with – to be either a victim or a Guardian – and that though he hated

165

the thought of being a Guardian, he couldn't endure being a victim any more. Only if he told her the truth about the Guardians could she come to understand him. And if he did that, she would hate him and he would lose her for sure.

All he could tell her was a lie. All that he could be to her was an invention, a fiction, another mask.

She said, not looking at him, 'I need some time to think, that's all.'

He said, 'Right. Fine. Whatever you think's best.'

He heard her say, 'I'm not saying I don't want to see you. I just mean – not for a bit, OK?'

He heard himself say, 'That's fine. Whatever you think's best.'

It was as if a gap was opening in the air between them, distancing them, severing them, until they could no longer see or hear each other properly. All he could do was stand and uselessly mouth words at her; all she could do was stand there and hear nothing.

Now they were just any two people talking.

He was unsurprised at how little emotion he felt. The cold and hard inside him had been growing and spreading for a long while now, until he had become almost totally pain-resistant – immune to feeling, to sensation, to caring.

He listened to her and heard himself speak to her for a short while more.

He watched her walk off.

He waited, knowing already, but somehow still wondering, to see if she would look back.

At the door to the science block she paused.

His heart didn't leap.

She opened the door, walked inside, let the door close after her.

After a long time, he moved away.

He was caught in a dream, trapped inside a memory. He knew it was a dream, and he wanted to be anywhere else, and he struggled to wake up – but it was no good.

He was back at his old school. On the worst day.

Last bell had gone. He was almost out of the gates. And then they grabbed him and took him to the changing rooms at the side of the school. Kevin Cunningham. John Sanders. Steven Watson. Any one of them was bad enough. The three together were beyond his worst imagining.

They held him with his back against the wall, pinning his arms. Kevin came up close, until his breath was on Elliot's face.

'Hello, Elliot. Were you thinking we'd forgotten you?'

He said nothing. Responding could only make it worse.

'Answer when you're spoken to.'

'No.'

'No what?'

'No – I hadn't forgotten you.'

'You're a loser, Elliot, you know that?'

'I . . . know that.'

Kevin smiled. 'There's a place for people like you, Elliot. It's called the rubbish tip. Why do you keep on turning up for school? You know we're always going to be waiting, ready to put you back where you belong.' He reached forward and ripped the front breast pocket of Elliot's blazer. It hung like a dead tongue.

Then he did the same to the other pockets.

For a moment, Elliot felt nothing. Then something inside him shifted. Suddenly, terrifyingly, like nothing he'd experienced before, white-hot rage erupted. It consumed him, uncontrollable, an exploding fire-storm, lunatic fury. He tore free of the hands pinning him and hurled himself at Kevin and hit him, hit him again, again, again –

I'll *kill* you, I'll *kill* you, *kill* you, *kill* you!

They wrenched him off and threw him against the wall. The back of his head smashed against the tiles, and he felt sick.

Slowly Kevin got up. He wiped blood off his mouth. 'You're going to wish you never did that.'

Elliot's rage was gone. Instead, he was blissfully numb. Everything was clear to him now. He would be dead very soon. But really, they'd already killed him a long time ago. So they couldn't hurt him any more.

He said, 'You can't kill me. I'm already dead.'

The first punch was right over his heart, and didn't hurt at all.

You can't hurt me. I'm dead already. Dead.

But then came the second punch, in the side of his head, and the third, right where the first one had landed.

Pretty soon it did hurt.

But you can't hurt me, he thought, *I'm dead already.*

It hurt more: a spreading pattern of warm pain.

Then a thermonuclear blast obliterated the top of his head, and he was falling, down, down. And mercifully, he died.

He wanted to wake up, but he was still inside the memory.

He remembered someone saying that you couldn't feel pain in dreams. They were wrong.

He didn't know how long he'd been dead or why he was back here now. The tiled floor was cold against his cheek. He let his tongue explore his swollen lips and poke into the hole where a tooth had come out. He didn't want to move anything else; so far, his body was a mass of numbness, and everything would be fine if it stayed that way. He carefully opened his eyes. Somewhere in his vision, blurring in and out of focus, was a copper pipe. He was in the shower room.

He watched the cloudy pink water flowing across the floor and into the drain. He thought, *It looks like cough mixture, like diluted cough mixture.* He thought of Kevin slowly emptying a bottle of cough mixture into the water. The laugh came up from inside him – he couldn't stop it, and he was forced to draw breath, to move, and the movement made something shift in his chest.

When the pain had receded slightly, he tried more careful movements. Breathing shallowly and not letting his chest bend, he got himself to his knees.

His clothes were underneath a shower. He realised that the roaring in his ears wasn't his blood surging round after all, but the noise of the water. He crawled over to them. The first thing he had to do was recover some decency by getting dressed, even if it killed him.

The realisation hit him like another nuclear blast. *I'm not dead at all.*

His T-shirt and shorts were sodden with sweat. The duvet was on the floor. The clock radio said 04:38.

He lay there, not moving.

What was it Louise had said about *Nineteen Eighty-Four*? *'To make him think like they wanted . . . they had to destroy him.'* It hadn't meant anything then, but now it did.

I survived. I survived being killed.

But inside, I was already dead.

But if you're dead, you can't feel. So maybe — maybe I wasn't then.

But how about now?

Chapter
17

The square of yellow paper was sandwiched between a call for new chess club members and an advert for the end-of-term swimming gala. To Elliot it appeared far larger than previous selection notices: conspicuous and accusing. Every time he passed the notice board he saw people around it.

The punishment was scheduled for tomorrow. It would be officially witnessed by Oliver, who would then report back to the Guardians. Guardians were never seen in the company of actual violence. Elliot supposed he should be thankful for that. It was far easier to make decisions when you didn't have to witness what those decisions did to people.

He moved through the day without effort, people and time and space flowing easily around him. He noticed something that until now he hadn't properly thought about: the world had no colours in it. He had assumed, because superficially it was obvious, that reality was made up of reds and yellows and greens and blues and purples – a rainbow's worth of colours. But in truth reality, when you looked – really looked – had more grey in it than anything else. Faces, people, walls, trees, sky – they were all made up of countless shades of grey.

The effect wasn't unpleasant, it just *was*. It didn't matter, it was just how things were. It did, however, make it more difficult to separate things. The greys leaked into each other, blurring edges and boundaries, making it not so obvious where one thing ended and another began. If he wasn't careful, there was a danger of forgetting that he had to distinguish his own, personal grey from all the other greys. He wondered what would happen if he did forget. Perhaps he, too, would blur and leak – perhaps his grey atoms would mingle with the other grey atoms until there was no longer any difference between the greys that made up the world and the grey that was him. No longer a world separate from him – just perpetual, endless grey.

Yes, that might be OK. That might be not unpleasant – if he cared about anything enough to mind one way or the other.

Back home, dinner was spaghetti bolognese. Once it had been his favourite food, now it was purely a substance to chew, swallow and digest. More greyness. They ate without talking, as they'd done every evening since *that* evening.

As soon as she'd finished eating, his mum got up and grabbed her coat from the hook on the door. 'I'm late for work – I'm working an extra half shift tonight. If it's not too much trouble,' – she drenched the words in acid – 'could you manage the washing up?'

When she'd gone, his dad stood up, his movements like an old man. Without looking at Elliot, he went into the lounge. Seconds later, Elliot heard the creak of his armchair and then the laughter of a studio audience – some rubbish game show.

He didn't hurry with the washing up, rinsing the plates and dishes carefully, filling the sink with very hot water, adding too much detergent. He scoured the plates, then tackled the remains of spaghetti bolognese welded to the bottom of the saucepan.

The water was scalding. He deliberately went more slowly, keeping his hands and wrists immersed. He focused on the heat, letting it hurt and burn, feeling it travel up his arms, spread out and intensify.

He pulled out his hands. The skin was red and angry. Pain wasn't grey. It was a reminder that at least part of him still existed. And pain helped block out everything else – including thinking about tomorrow's punishment.

Later he mechanically brushed his teeth and packed his school bag. He remembered he needed a towel for swimming practice, and went back downstairs to grab one from the airing cupboard in the kitchen. The living room light was still on, although there was no sound from the TV. His dad must have gone to bed and forgotten to turn it off. Elliot went in to turn it off himself and saw that although the TV was dead his dad was sitting in his chair – or, rather, slumped in it, which was why he'd been invisible from the doorway.

His dad was asleep, his chest rising and falling, his face trembling slightly with each breath.

Elliot looked at him – at the receding greying hair pushed back by ragged triangles of scalp, at the folds under his eyes, the weight of the skin pulling down the shape of his face. Remembering.

You can do anything if you put your mind to it.

Then why didn't you, Dad? Why didn't you put your mind to it and get better? Why did you just give up and leave us?

I followed your advice, though. I put my mind to it. I got all the way. Right to the top. What would you say to that, Dad, if you knew? 'That's the way – that's the only way'?

But he couldn't feel anger any more. Or hate. Or anything.

Who are we? he thought. *Me and Mum and you? Do I know us at all any more?*

He was suddenly desperately tired. He wanted to leave, go to bed, obliterate everything. But his legs were plasticine – he didn't have the strength to walk upstairs or even out of the room. He managed to stumble to the sofa. He collapsed on to it and closed his eyes.

Please let me never wake up. That way, all this will go away. Or let me wake up and make it four years ago. Let it never be tomorrow. Please.

'Elliot?'

Someone was calling him.

'Elliot?'

'Uuum.' Elliot struggled to consciousness. His eyes were sore, gritty, his arms and legs heavy and lifeless.

His mum was bending over him. She shook his shoulder again. Her face was blurred. She smelt of the old people's home: lasagne, floor polish and stale lavender.

'I've put the kettle on,' she said. 'What do you want?'

He shook his head drowsily. 'S'OK. Tired. Need to sleep.' He looked over at his dad's chair. Empty.

'He's in bed,' his mum said. 'Where you and I should be. But I want us to have a talk. Now, tea, coffee or chocolate?'

He couldn't focus his mind enough to answer.

'Hot chocolate,' she said. 'It'll do us both good.'

She went through to the kitchen. Elliot fought to wake up fully. As his brain churned sluggishly into motion, currents of panic began to circulate. *What 'talk'? What about?*

She came back in with two mugs, handed one to Elliot, then sat at the opposite end of the sofa.

They said nothing for a while. Elliot focused on his mug of chocolate. He wondered if he was expected to start off the conversation.

Abruptly his mum started talking. 'I thought it would be enough, coming here. New house, new school, new town. New start. Now . . .' She sighed. 'I don't know. Doesn't seem to have worked out all that well, does it?'

Elliot guessed it was one of those questions that wasn't intended to elicit a response. And if it was supposed to, what was he supposed to say anyway?

'Elliot?'

He knew she was looking at him, willing him to look at her. He didn't want to. He wanted her to shut up and let him go to bed before he said something he didn't mean in order to make her leave him alone.

'Elliot. Look at me. Please.'

He looked but at the same time didn't look, concentrating on the patch of skin between her eyes – the trick Richard had taught him.

She was smiling – a sad smile. 'Seems a long time ago that we last talked,' she said. 'Properly, I mean. Suddenly you look – different. More grown up, I suppose. Not the –' She looked down. 'I couldn't expect you never to change.'

Oh, I'm different all right. You wouldn't believe how different I am.

The smile slipped. 'I don't blame you if you're angry with me, Elliot. I've had so much to do, so much else to worry about – keeping some money coming in, looking after your dad, everything – I just hoped you'd be able to sort yourself out. I'm sorry. I really am.'

I could make you angry as well as sorry, he thought tiredly. *I could make you wish you'd never asked me. I could make you go away and cry. I'm good at doing that to people. Haven't you heard? Please don't make me do it to you. Just leave me alone.*

'Please, Elliot. I can't bear seeing you in this state. Bottling everything up, the same as you did before. I won't let that happen all over again. Can't you see that?'

'It was different then.' He'd intended to say it casually, nonchalantly, brutally – like Richard would have been able to do. But the words choked in his throat and instead came out in a croaking whisper. He gulped the hot chocolate, the thick liquid sliding greasily down his throat.

'No, it's not different.' Her voice trembled. 'It's not different at all. A lot of things have changed, but I'm still the woman who gave birth to you, who's watched you live and grow, and you're still my son, still part of me. That doesn't change, whatever else does. And that means I'm not going to let you push me away – I'm not going to give up that easily, so don't think I will.'

Her voice tore at him, blackmailed him. He tried to shut it out, pretend he couldn't hear her, wasn't listening to her. *I'm not here. You're not here. Get lost. Leave me alone.* To his horror he found he was crying, tears spilling down his face unbidden, and he didn't have the energy to fight them back or even wipe them away.

I am strong. I am strong. I am –

He felt her take the mug out of his hands, then sit down next to him. She drew his head towards her until it was resting on her shoulder. He felt his crying soaking the sleeve of her dress, but couldn't move, couldn't do anything but sit and let her hold him as if he was a small child again.

'Please, Elliot. Wouldn't it be better if you told me what was wrong?

'Are you – is it school? Only – if you're being bullied again –'

It would have been wonderful, so wonderful, if he could have answered 'yes'.

She gently combed her fingers through his hair, making little *tch* sounds. 'Why do you have to use all this gel? It makes your hair all dry and horrible.' But she said it as if she didn't mean it, as if it was simply something to say, and she didn't stop her fingers moving.

He took a deep, shuddering breath. 'I can't tell you. You'd hate me. You'd hate me for what I've done.'

'I won't hate you, whatever it is. I could never hate you.'

'You think that now.'

'I'll always think that. Whatever you've done, I won't give up on you. The same as I will never give up on your dad. Surely you know that?'

He wanted to say, *That's not true, is it, that middle bit?* 'That's not – I didn't think you – you and Dad – That's not what it looks like from here.'

She was quiet for a moment, and he thought he'd said the wrong thing and that she was angry again.

Then she said, 'I'm not going to pretend there aren't – I don't know how many days I want to give it all up and leave and get out and truly start all over again. But your dad did everything he could for us when he was able . . . and now he's not, through no fault of his own, it's my turn to do everything I can for him. Which – which might include screaming and shouting and – That's how it works. At least, that's how I *want* it to work. We've got through things so far, helped each other so far, and I can't let all that go. Not without a fight. For me, it's like your dad says: "That's the way – that's the only way." '

He said, croakily, 'It's not the same with me, though, is it?'

'Isn't it? I don't know. If you won't tell me, only you can know that.'

'It isn't. It's not like that. I'm able. I just – I just can't make myself stop it. I want to – I want to make it all stop – but whatever I do – I can't stop being scared, and then –' He stopped, terrified that if he went on it would all flood out.

For a while, all he could hear was his own breathing.

'Sometimes –' She hesitated, 'sometimes, other people can help you with your battles. But if they can't – or for some reason you won't let them – and you think you're on your own, fighting can be the hardest thing on earth. And nothing I can say is going to make whatever you need to do any easier. But I want you to understand this: I will never give up on you. Not while I'm still standing and breathing.

'Do you understand?

'Whatever happens, whatever you've done, I will *never* give up on you.'

18

He got up early, showered, dressed and went down to the kitchen. He managed a cup of tea for breakfast, but couldn't face eating.

He swilled out his mug and went quietly upstairs. He picked up his school bag from his bedroom, hesitated, then put it down. He went back downstairs and outside, closing the front door behind him.

When he reached the school there were a handful of small kids playing football in the playground – probably from one of the buses that picked up from outside the town. They stopped and watched him as he walked past them.

Do you know who I am? he thought. *Do you know what I could make happen to you? Do you know that you should be afraid of me?*

He looked away from them and went on towards the main school building.

Inside he glanced at the notice board, saw the small square of yellow paper nestled between the other notices. His stomach tightened, but he walked on down the corridor.

He still had the chance to change his mind – to not do it. He tried to push the thought away.

I can still go back. I can still turn around, walk out of here, save myself.

The fear rose.

There had been chances before, every step of the way. But every step of the way he'd had to fight his fear. And every step of the way the fear had won.

He didn't know why it should be any different now.

The voice might have told him, but the voice was silent. It wasn't going to help – or hinder.

His footfalls echoed off the wood-panelled walls, off the glass-fronted portraits of former headmasters, off the hi-tech plastic floor. The noise was like laughter, mocking him.

Go away, little boy. How can you think you can do anything? We have history to defend us; you have only yourself.

His stomach cramped violently, making him lurch and almost fall. He tried to lock his insides together.

What am I doing? he thought. He knew he couldn't do it. He didn't have the strength to stand up to one person, never mind the Guardians. The Guardians and all the forces they commanded or that otherwise served them. Power. Violence. Fear.

We didn't create Holminster, Elliot. Holminster created us.

He knew he possessed strength of a kind; the strength that had enabled him to become – almost – a Guardian. For good or bad it was part of him. But it wasn't the kind of strength he needed now. Now he needed a strength that would enable him to forfeit the first kind of strength. The strength that allowed you to stop a handhold below the summit of Everest, lean back into emptiness – and let go.

I've never had that kind of strength. Never.

Too quickly, the headmaster's door was in front of him. He fought the urge to run for the toilets and be sick.

He closed his eyes. Tried to fortify himself. Silently repeated the words from last night: *I will never give up on you. Do you understand? Whatever happens, whatever you've done . . .*

But you can't help me here, he thought. *It's like you said – some battles you have to fight alone.*

No one can help me here.

He saw again the figure held against the tiled wall of the changing room. Saw again Kevin's fists pounding, over and over. Saw again the body on the floor, broken and bleeding.

His chest tightened. It was hard to take a breath.

Life or death, he thought. *That's the choice. And who would choose death?*

He realised he already knew the answer.

I would. I'm dead already.

He had pushed away and cut himself off from every-thing that mattered – everyone he cared for and who cared for him.

I'm dead already.

Yet, he suddenly saw, at the same time part of him had chosen not to die. The old Elliots – the Elliots he'd done his utmost to kill – had stubbornly clung on to life. Must have, because he was still afraid.

Not dying after all my efforts, he thought. *That, surely, takes strength.*

Before he could lose the moment, he raised his arm to knock –

He hesitated.

The school was quiet. The only sound came from behind the door: a cough, the faint shuffle of papers. But something had made him stop.

And then he knew what it was. His mouth was dry as tissue paper, his stomach had all but dissolved, sourness rose in his throat – and yet, despite all that, he was . . . calm. That was the word: not good, not happy, but calm. A deep, strong, quiet calm he had never experienced before.

He thought, *I'm afraid, but I'm still going through with it.*

He didn't remember ever being able to do that before.

It made him think of Louise, and Ben.

I could tell you, now, who I really am, if you wanted to know me after this.

What was it Louise had said when she'd talked about the hero in *Nineteen Eighty-Four*? She'd said, 'He chooses to disobey the system. He obeys what he believes and risks everything. So he makes himself free . . .' He hadn't understood it at the time, but he did now. It meant that what was important, what mattered, was not the fact of being afraid but rather what you did, the choices you made, when you were afraid. And maybe that was something to do with being alive – or staying dead.

He would have liked to dwell longer on the thought, but now was not the right time. He knew, somehow, that it would not lose itself easily.

He brought his hand up again, and this time he didn't hesitate.